HARD BARGAIN

HARD BARGAIN

THE BRANDON HALL SERIES BOOK 2

MIKE RYAN

WWW.MIKERYANBOOKS.COM

Copyright © 2020 by Mike Ryan

All rights reserved.

No part of this book may be reproduced in any form or by any electronic or mechanical means, including information storage and retrieval systems, without written permission from the author, except for the use of brief quotations in a book review.

Book Cover: Warren Design

1

Hall came home to his apartment, a little depressed about being turned down again. He'd applied for loans at several banks, all of them said he needed to build up his credit history before being granted a loan to start his trucking business. He sat down on his couch, drinking a beer, feeling sorry for himself. This wasn't exactly how he pictured things going when he left the service. Though he was able to get a small loan because of his veteran status, it wasn't enough to buy a few trucks, a warehouse for storage, plus all the other costs of starting a new business. He needed a larger loan.

Though not everything in Hall's life was going to plan, he couldn't say it was all going badly. It'd been two months since he met Charlotte, and things had been going pretty well between them. They'd started dating exclusively and were really enjoying being with each other. Hall had sent her a message on the way home, letting her know he was turned down again. Today was one of her work-at-home days, so she scurried down the hall only a few minutes after Hall arrived.

They were at the stage where they didn't bother knocking, so Charlotte barged right in, going over to Hall and giving him a hug and a kiss. She sat next to him and held him for a few minutes, hoping to cheer him up.

"It's OK," Charlotte said. "You'll get what you need. It's just gonna take a little longer than you figured."

"Maybe it wasn't meant to be. Maybe I should've just picked something smaller to start out with."

"Brandon, don't give up already. You just need to give it a little more time."

"Yeah, I guess, but I have to start doing something soon. I can't just sit around all the time watching old cartoons all day."

Charlotte wasn't sure this was the best time to spring some of the news she had, but she'd been thinking about it for a few days now and didn't want to wait any longer. Besides, she figured talking about something else would help put Hall in a better mood. At least it would give him something different to think about, which maybe wouldn't depress him so much.

"Uh...," Charlotte said, unsure of how to begin, "I was thinking..."

Hall broke free of Charlotte's grasp and looked

strangely at her, sensing that she had something on her mind. "What's the matter? What is it?"

"Oh, well, nothing's the matter. I was just... I, uh..."

"You know, in all the time we've known each other, which admittedly hasn't been that long, whenever you've started sentences without completing them, and you say uh a lot, you have something you want to say that you're not sure how I'm going to react to."

Charlotte nervously smiled, then let out a small giggle. "Uh, yeah, I kind of noticed that myself."

"So what is it?"

"It's uh... well..."

"If you've found another guy or something, or you wanna go more slowly, it's fine, just say so, I can handle it. Really, I won't scream and holler. Much. At least until after you leave, and then I might put a few holes in the wall, but it's fine. I can take it."

Charlotte smiled, then put her hands on both sides of his face and leaned in to give him a more passionate kiss, hoping to put his mind at ease. "It's nothing like that. Really? You really thought there might be someone else?"

Hall shrugged. "No, not really. Just figured with my luck lately, that maybe... well, you know the saying: when it rains it pours."

"Well, it's nothing like that. I promise. I love you, and I love being with you."

Charlotte then realized what she said and quickly looked away and cleared her throat. An uncomfortable look came over Hall's face as well, thinking she may have just spilled the secret. Though they'd been growing very fond of each other, neither had yet told the other that they loved them. Hall's heart started beating heavy, thinking if that's what she had on her mind, he wasn't sure what he was going to say in response. It was a very awkward moment for the both of them. Charlotte didn't intend for those words to slip out of her lips. While she was sure she meant them, and it was something that had crossed her mind on more than one occasion recently, she thought it might have been too soon to say them. Especially since Hall didn't seem like he was ready for it. Seeing the look on his face pretty much led her to believe she was right in that aspect. He looked like he wanted to be anywhere other than there at that moment.

Before continuing any further, Charlotte figured she had several options. One was to ignore what she said and tell him what was really on her mind, pretending the words never left her lips. Another option was to expound on what she said and open a different, and much deeper, conversation than she originally intended. The last option she thought of was to acknowledge what she said, but not make a big deal out of it, and just quickly move on to another topic so as not to embarrass either one of them any further. She chose the first option. Considering they both seemed uncomfortable now, it was best to just sweep it under the rug and pretend it was never said.

Charlotte cleared her throat as she continued her original thoughts. "Uh, anyway, um...". She let out an uncomfortable sounding laugh. "I almost forgot what I was gonna say."

Hall put his hands in his lap and fiddled with his fingers, still nervously waiting to hear what was on her mind. "Take your time."

Charlotte ran her hands through her hair, still clearly embarrassed about what she'd said. She felt uncomfortable and imagined that Hall was looking through her, his eyes burning as he tried to figure out how to respond to her unwelcomed words. Charlotte felt like the walls were starting to close in.

"Umm, you know what? I think I, um, I, uh, forgot something in my apartment. I'll be back a little later."

By now, Hall could see that she seemed more uncomfortable and uneasy than he was. "Charlotte."

Hall reached for her hand, but Charlotte didn't let him grab it and walked toward the door.

"It's just work stuff," Charlotte said. "I'll, uh, I'll be back."

Hall watched her leave and couldn't help but feel responsible for her leaving. It must have been his fault, he thought. When she said she loved him, the most excruciating look must have come over his face, causing her to severely backpedal and question herself. If he would have just acted cool, then she wouldn't have felt the way she did and rushed off. He took another sip of his beer, wishing he could start the day all over again. Hall sighed, took a few more swallows of his drink, before putting it down on the table. He got up, knowing he had to go comfort Charlotte and tell her something, anything. He wasn't sure what yet, but something to let her know that it wasn't her.

Hall exited his apartment and went down the hall to Charlotte's place. He tried to open the door, but it was locked. Luckily, they'd exchanged spare keys a few weeks prior to that. Hall reached inside his pants pocket to remove the key and unlocked the door. As soon as he opened it, Hall could immediately hear the muffled sounds of a woman crying. He closed the door behind him and took a few steps, seeing Charlotte lying there on the couch, face down, crying into a throw pillow.

Hall walked over to her, Charlotte still not acknowledging his presence, either because she didn't know he was there, or because she was ignoring him. He sat down on the couch and grabbed her arms to sit her up straight. He put his arms around her, Charlotte burying her head into his chest.

"How'd you get in here? I thought I locked it?"

"You did," Hall answered. "Did you forget we exchanged keys?"

"Oh, yeah. I forgot. I guess because we haven't used them yet."

"Well, you've never locked me out before either."

"True."

Hall held Charlotte's face in his hands and wiped away her tears. "Why are you crying?"

Charlotte shrugged. "I guess because I was making a fool of myself."

"You weren't."

"Yes, I was. Don't try to lie just to make me feel better."

Hall smiled. "I'm not lying."

"Yes, you are. But it's OK. I'm, uh... I'm sorry."

"For what? You don't have anything to apologize for."

"For saying I... you know. For saying what I said."

"Why are you saying sorry for that?" Hall asked.

"Because I could see by your reaction that you don't... that you're not ready for that type of thing. I actually didn't even mean to say it. It just kind of came out."

Hall gently held her chin with his thumb and index finger, then leaned in and tenderly kissed her lips. "So you didn't mean it?"

"What?"

"You didn't mean what you said?"

"Well, no, I mean, yeah, of course I meant the words," Charlotte said. "I just didn't mean to say them right now."

"Why not?"

"Because I just... I know that you're not... can we please just drop this?"

"No, we need to talk about it," Hall replied.

"Why? Let's just let it go and move on and forget I ever said it."

"Why would I wanna do that? If we did that, then you wouldn't know that... I love you too."

Charlotte almost didn't hear what he said, letting out a cough before realizing the words he'd just said quickly. She sat there paralyzed, before slowly turning her face back to him.

"What'd you just say?"

Hall smiled, thinking she was just doing it for effect. "You really need me to say it again?"

"I want to make sure I heard you correctly."

"I said that I... love you too."

It didn't get quite the reaction that Hall was hoping for. Instead of looking happy and smiling, and maybe giving him a few hugs, some passionate kisses, it was just the opposite. She huffed and shook her head, her frown going even further in that downward direction. He wasn't sure what he did wrong. There was a disconnect somewhere between hearing the words in his own head and what must have been muttered through his mouth.

"What?" Hall asked, looking bewildered.

"No, no, don't do that."

Hall put his arms up, completely clueless. "Don't do what?"

"Don't do that. Don't just tell me something like that because it's what you think I want to hear. Don't do that. That's beneath you. You're a better guy than that."

Hall pulled his head back like he was offended. "I'm telling you the truth."

"Listen, I said what I said, and now it's out there, and if you're not ready for it, that's fine. But I don't need or want you saying that just to appease me. I want you to say it when you really feel it, when you really mean it."

Hall leaned in closer to give her another kiss. "I do mean it. I wouldn't say it if I didn't." He kissed her again. "I do love you."

"You do?"

Hall nodded.

"You're not just saying that?"

Hall shook his head.

"Would you have said it if I didn't?" she asked.

Hall moved his face around like he had just eaten something sour. "Yeah, probably not. But that doesn't change the fact that I do. I guess I was just surprised, not expecting to hear that right now. But like I said, it doesn't change that I feel the same way about you."

Charlotte finally smiled, a rush of happiness flowing through her body. She planted a kiss on Hall's lips, quickly followed by several more. After kissing for a few minutes, Hall begrudgingly broke his lips free from hers, as hard a thing as that was to do.

"What's the matter?" Charlotte asked.

"Nothing. I just remembered... didn't you have something else you wanted to talk to me about?"

"Huh? Oh, yeah, I almost forgot."

"You did forget."

"Well, it was your fault."

"Uh... OK, I'll take the blame on that," Hall said. "Anyway, what was it?"

"Well, it was a couple things. One of which was us."

"Us? Outside of what we just said, what else could it be? I mean, I know you're not pregnant or anything, so that can't be it."

"Ha, funny. Obviously not. But it could change things for us."

"Oh, really?" Hall asked, looking a little worried.

"It's nothing bad. At least I hope not. Just different."

2

"So what's this all about?" Hall warily asked.

"OK, so, first of all, there's two separate things. One's personal. One's business."

"Business?"

"Yes. So which one would you like to hear first?"

"Umm, I'm not sure I really wanna hear either."

Charlotte laughed. "I promise you it's nothing bad."

"OK. Why don't you just surprise me then? Start off with whatever you want."

Charlotte thought about it for a second and figured it'd be better to save the personal stuff for last. That would probably be the bigger bombshell. Not to mention the fact that she was nervous about mentioning it to him.

"I'll start with our business."

"Our business?" Hall said.

"Yes. Since you've been having trouble getting your

trucking business started, I thought maybe we could steer off course a little bit."

"Off course how?"

Charlotte faked a cough. "Well, since we did such a good job with that other little incident that brought us together, I thought we could start our own private investigation business."

A surprised look came over Hall's face. His eyes widened and his eyebrows raised. "What'd you say?" Even though he heard Charlotte clearly, he was sure she had to be making some kind of joke.

"Why don't we start our own private investigation business?"

Hall continued to look at her like she was crazy. "You can't be serious."

"Why not? Between the two of us, we should be able to handle things."

"Huh? We should? Do you know what you're saying?"

"I do," Charlotte answered. "I've been looking into it for a week or so, and I think we can do it."

"First of all, I'm not really interested. Second of all, what's with the *we* stuff?"

"We can do it together as a team. You and me. I know marketing and design, so I can do a lot of the office stuff while you're out on a case, and then on occasion when you need extra help, I can back you up out there."

"You can?"

"Yeah. What do you think?"

"I think you've lost your mind," Hall replied. "You make it sound like it'll be a piece of cake or something."

"Well, we've already handled one big incident. They're all not gonna be like that. Most of it's going to be pretty mundane, I'm sure."

"Oh, I'm sure."

"You don't like it?"

"We almost got killed you know. Multiple times," he said.

"Yeah, but we didn't. We made it, got some experience, and now we'll be better and know some things on what not to do."

"Where in the world did you come up with all this?" Hall asked.

Charlotte shrugged. "I don't know. Just kind of came to me. I was trying to figure out how to help you, and in doing that, was trying to think of what kind of business best suited your skills."

"And this is what you came up with?"

"It was either that, or open up some kind of martial arts school, or be a bodyguard."

"And all that didn't appeal to you?"

"Well, I figured you'd have the same problem getting a loan for the school, and the bodyguard I immediately ruled out because I don't want you guarding anyone else's body, especially any rich, attractive females."

Hall smiled. "Makes perfect sense."

"I thought so."

"It's not gonna be that easy, you know. There aren't frying pans lying around just waiting for you to use it on somebody."

"Ha, ha, very funny. I'm never gonna live that down, am I?"

"Probably not."

"Just don't shoot the idea down without thinking about it, please."

"Charlotte, I really appreciate you trying to help me, but when I left the service, I wanted to do something nonviolent."

"Well, it doesn't have to be violent. Most of it's just following people, investigating, talking, things like that."

"I'm sure you can't just put up a website and call yourself a private investigator without some kind of license or form or something."

Charlotte fake-coughed again. "Well, I kind of happened to stumble over the qualifications earlier and…"

"Just happened to stumble on them, huh?"

"Yes, let me finish. You have to get fingerprinted, there's an application packet, an exam, you have to get insurance, and, oh, yeah, you have to have a couple years' experience."

"Just stumbled on it?" Charlotte flashed him that sexy smile of hers that had a way of melting him. "I don't have a couple years' experience, and I'm not particularly interested in working for somebody else to get it. I wanted to do my own thing, start my own business, work for me."

"You still can. You worked as an MP, right?"

"For a couple years."

"That qualifies as meeting the experience requirement."

"Charlotte, I worked as an MP for three years before qualifying and transferring into Ranger school. Very few people ever do that or are accepted. You know why I wanted to do that?"

Charlotte shook her head.

"Because I hated being an MP. I couldn't wait to get out of there."

"Oh. So does that mean you're not even the slightest bit interested?"

Hall threw his arms up. "I dunno. I mean... I got out of the service because I wanted to do something different. This wouldn't seem all that different, would it?"

"Well, it kinda is." Charlotte's happy face slowly started turning back into a frown. Hall hated thinking he was disappointing her again.

"Don't get me wrong, I really appreciate you trying to help me, I really do. I love that you're trying to look out for me, but, I just... I don't know."

"Why don't you give it a chance?"

"Why are you pushing this so much? Seems a little out of character for you."

"Uh, well, I sort of might have our first case if you decide you want to do it."

"You sort of have our first case?" Hall asked. "Is that sort of like having money in your wallet?"

"Well, I told this girl that we would look into something for her. Now if you don't want to do it, that's fine, I won't force you, or make you do something you don't want to do, so if that's the case, then I'll just do it myself, no problem."

"You told who?"

"This girl I know from a previous job. We've kept in touch the last few years, and when I heard what happened, I reached out to her."

"Heard about what?"

"Her brother died," Charlotte answered.

"Oh. I'm sorry to hear that."

"Yeah. Apparently, the police said it was a drug overdose, but she doesn't think so."

"Why not?"

"She said her brother didn't do drugs. She thinks he was murdered and someone was trying to cover it up."

"Charlotte..."

She could already anticipate his objections. "I know what you're gonna say, that we shouldn't get involved, that it's not our business, but she could really use our help."

"A lot of people are in denial when they find out a

close friend or family member was doing something that they shouldn't or didn't think they did."

"She swears he was not into drugs."

"It's the shock of the situation," Hall said. "It's tough to accept at first."

"Yeah, I know, and I had a feeling you would say something like that."

"I'm sure the police know what they're doing."

"I'm sure. Anyway, I agreed to meet her later tonight after she's done work."

"You what?"

"I'm going to meet her to talk about it. I told you, if you don't want to get involved, that's fine, but I still feel like I'm going to help."

Hall lowered his face and started scratching the top of his head, not very pleased with her news. "You're gonna investigate this thing by yourself?"

"Sure am."

"Even though the police already said what it was?"

"Yep."

Hall loudly sighed as he looked away. Charlotte let out a small grin, knowing she was wearing him down, though she quickly wiped the look off her face so as not to give the impression that she was trapping him. After a few seconds, Hall turned his attention back to his lovely girlfriend.

"I can't let you do this."

"Well, I am," Charlotte replied. "My friend insists

that something's not right, and I'm gonna find out what it is."

"You don't know anything about investigating."

Charlotte cleared her throat. "Ahem. What do you think we did before?"

"Would you stop referencing everything that happened after the train? It was an isolated incident. We were on the run for our lives. This is completely different."

"How?"

Hall stopped for a moment to think. "Because this time we would be knowingly thrusting ourselves into a bad situation instead of it being forced upon us."

"Doesn't change the fact that we could do it."

Hall sighed loudly again, clearly displeased. "You're really gonna do this?"

"Sure am."

"You're gonna force me to do this, aren't you?"

Charlotte innocently batted her eyes at him. "I'm not forcing you to do anything. I said I would do it on my own."

"Yeah, and likely get killed in the process."

"I'll be fine."

"You'll be fine," Hall mumbled under his breath. "I can't believe I'm gonna get roped into this."

"What was that?"

"I said I'll go with you."

"You don't have to do that. I'm perfectly capable of doing it on my own."

"And can I ask you a question?"

"Sure."

"What are you gonna do if you investigate this thing by yourself and run into a situation where you're in a fight and have to fend off three or four guys by yourself?"

"I'm sure I'll manage," Charlotte replied.

"You can't pull a frying pan out of your pocket."

"Will you stop with the frying pan thing?"

"OK, OK."

"Brandon, it's fine, I don't mind doing it on my own if you're not interested."

Hall rolled his eyes. "No, I'll go with you on one condition."

"Which is?"

"If I'm not satisfied that this friend of yours is actually on to something, we drop it. Both of us."

"But if she is, then you'll help?"

Hall sighed and curled his lips, not really looking forward to the proposition. "Yeah."

Charlotte finally let a wide smile show on her face as she excitedly clapped her hands in front of her. She then thrust herself on Hall, giving him a big hug, almost knocking him over.

"This'll work out. I promise."

"We'll see," Hall said.

"So do you think this could be the start of a whole new thing for us?"

"Let's just see how this turns out first, huh?"

"OK." Charlotte gave him a kiss. "Thank you for coming with me."

"I knew I should've shoved a different girl back into her apartment."

"Hey!" Charlotte playfully punched him in the shoulder, the two of them rolling around on the couch, kissing and hugging.

"So what's the other thing?"

"What?"

"The other thing," Hall said. "You said you had a business and personal thing to ask. What's the personal thing?"

"Oh. You know, now's probably not the best time to talk about it. We can do it later."

"Oh, no. You're not doing that."

"Saying something and then dropping it, making me wonder for days or weeks what you were going to say, making me go out of my mind thinking about whether it's something bad."

"It's not bad. I promise."

"Then you shouldn't mind telling me now."

"I'm not sure I want to now."

"Charlotte, just say it."

"Do I have to?"

"If you want me to visit this friend of yours, then yes. I'm making that one of the conditions."

"That's not fair. You already said you were going."

"I altered the agreement."

"That's really not fair."

Hall shrugged. "It is what it is. So if you want me to go, you need to spill it."

Now it was Charlotte's turn to sigh, wondering why she ever mentioned it to begin with. She was having severe second thoughts.

"OK. Promise me you won't freak out or anything?"

Hall rolled his head back. He knew that was never a good sign when someone prefaced whatever they were about to say with that line.

"Promise?" Charlotte repeated.

Hall let out a deep breath, mentally trying to prepare himself for anything. "I promise."

"Do I really have to do this?"

"You're the one who brought it up to begin with," he said.

"Yeah, but can I just change my mind?"

"No. Say it."

"Fine." She stroked her hair for a moment, then rubbed her face, seemingly doing everything possible to delay what was on her mind. Hall could tell that she was obviously nervous about whatever was going to come out of her lips. "OK. So I was thinking…"

"That's a good start."

Charlotte laughed, then playfully slapped his arm. "Will you let me finish?"

"OK, I promise."

"Uh, well, since you don't have work right now, and since we're mostly with each other all the time now anyway, and, um, you know... since we've been together a couple months now... if..."

Hall moved his head closer to her and moved his hand around to help spur her on as she stopped mid-sentence, almost like she forgot what she was going to say, though he knew it was because she seemed embarrassed to say. "Yes?"

Charlotte continued, though she talked in a very low voice. "If, um, if... you wanted to move in... together?"

Hall gulped, definitely not ready for that question. He wasn't sure what was going to come out of her mouth, but he didn't think that was going to be one of the options. He seemed stunned, not quite as much as when he heard she loved him, but still taken aback just the same.

"Uh, well, it's kind of soon for that, don't you think?" Hall asked.

"Yeah, maybe. I just figured why pay rent for two when we can do it for one? Plus, we're together most of the time anyway, and assuming neither of us is planning on dumping the other anytime soon, I thought maybe... I dunno, now that I actually said it out loud instead of just inside my head, I guess it does sound kind of silly, doesn't it?"

"Doesn't sound silly at all."

"Just forget I mentioned it."

"Why? You don't want to?"

"Well, no, I mean, yeah, I mean... I know it's probably a little early to be talking about, so we can just put it aside for a while if you want."

"Do you need an answer right now?" Hall asked.

"No. It was too soon, wasn't it?"

"It's fine."

"You don't want to, I can tell."

"It's not that."

"What is it then?"

"It's just... everything is going really good between us, if we change things... I just don't want to screw it up."

"Nothing would really change other than where we're sleeping, but I totally get it, and I'm not gonna push or anything, so if you're not ready, I totally understand."

"I'm definitely not against the idea or anything," Hall said. "I just want to make sure we're in a good enough spot that we can overcome any bumps in the road."

"Such as?"

"Uh, I dunno, like, I like to do laundry at night, you like to do it during the day. I like to leave dishes in the sink for a few hours, you like to put them in the dishwasher right away, just small things like that that don't really matter, but maybe can grate on another person's nerves."

"I don't think that would be a problem."

"Maybe not. I just wanna be sure."

"And I'm OK with that," Charlotte said. "Just think

about it for a while and let me know when you'll be ready. If you ever are."

"You can scratch the if off. I'm not gonna be one of those guys who's afraid of commitment or of getting closer or anything. It's not gonna be ten years in the same situation. I just wanna make sure it's right."

"OK. I respect that."

"Thank you."

Hall leaned over and gave her another kiss. After kissing for a few moments, Charlotte regretfully had to tear herself away to start getting ready. Hall watched her go from her bedroom to the bathroom several times before curiosity finally got the better of him.

"What are you doing?" Hall asked.

"Getting ready to leave."

"For where?"

"I told you," Charlotte replied. "We were going to see my friend about her brother. You should probably change into something more comfortable too instead of that suit you're wearing."

"Right now?"

"Yeah. I told her we'd get there in about an hour."

"An hour? I thought you said later?"

"Well, an hour is later, isn't it?" Charlotte said with a smirk.

"Didn't leave yourself much room to hoodwink me into this, did you?"

"I didn't hoodwink you. You're free to do whatever you want."

"Yeah, yeah, so you say."

"Just remember, it's for a good cause. Olivia's a good person, and she's genuinely upset about her brother. It's not like you're going to see someone about losing a stamp collection or something."

"I just hope we don't get in over our head."

3

Hall and Charlotte arrived at her friend's place, a two bed, two bath condo on the outskirts of Anaheim. It was a small place, but big enough for a young, single woman who only had to take care of herself and a cat that preferred to be left alone, anyway. Olivia Zeller was sitting in a rocker on the front porch, eagerly waiting for her guests to come. Once she saw them get out of the car after they arrived, she sprinted across the small lawn in order to give Charlotte a hug upon reaching her.

"Thank you so much for coming," Zeller whispered in her ear.

Charlotte cradled the back of her friend's head. "It's no problem. I just hope we can help."

"I have to admit, I was a little afraid that you wouldn't come."

"Of course I would."

After the two friends ended their embrace and took a few steps away from each other, Zeller noticed the athletically well-built man standing behind Charlotte looking on.

"That him?" Zeller asked.

"Yes." Charlotte turned around and waved at Hall to come closer.

Hall plastered a smile on his face and pulled his hand up, only two of his fingers along with his thumb actually standing up as he delivered a half-hearted sort of a wave. "Hi."

"Hello," Zeller said. "Thank you for coming. Let's go inside and talk."

The three of them went inside the condo and sat down in the living room. After Zeller gave the pair something to drink, they quickly got down to business.

"So you're the ex-army guy?" Zeller asked.

"Yeah, I guess so," Hall said.

With him not sounding very excited to be there, Charlotte spoke up for him. "He doesn't like to talk about it."

"Oh, OK. So I'm going to be your first case, huh?"

Charlotte looked at her partner and still saw no expression on his face. "Well, we did have one previous… uh… situation."

Hall and Charlotte glanced at each other, him giving her the fakest smile he could muster.

"Well, I'm just glad you've come," Zeller said. "The police aren't doing anything else; they've closed the case. I just... I don't know what else to do or who else to turn to."

Charlotte turned her head toward Hall again, making a face that could only be seen by him, one that screamed at him silently to start speaking up. Hall didn't like the look she was giving him and cleared his throat, finally ready to do his part.

"Umm, why don't you just start at the beginning?" Hall said. "Why do you feel that your brother was murdered, and it wasn't an overdose?"

"Because he didn't do drugs," Zeller answered. "I mean, ever."

Hall raised an eyebrow at the remark. "Never?"

"I mean, he smoked some pot back in high school, but it was only like once or twice a month, and that was only when he was with some friends. He just wasn't that into it."

"Charlotte told me the police found needle marks in his arm."

"That's what doesn't make any sense. That's not him. He didn't do that stuff."

"How can you be sure?" Hall asked. "Was he living here?"

"No, he was living with a couple of roommates in an apartment in some off-campus housing. Just a couple blocks away from school."

"I don't mean to be unsympathetic to your loss or anything, and I'm deeply sorry for that, but I don't understand how you can be so sure that your brother wasn't into anything if you weren't there."

"Because I saw my brother two days before he was killed. He was wearing a short-sleeved shirt, and we were sitting at my kitchen table, having dinner, talking for hours. I would've noticed if there were marks in his arm. There weren't."

"But..."

"I once dated a guy for a few months who did some hard drugs from time to time, and he shoved some things into his arms, so I know what the marks would look like if they were there."

Hall looked away for a second, not wanting to sound like a complete jerk knowing that was probably how he was coming across anyway. Nevertheless, they were hard questions, and they needed to be asked.

"I'm not trying to doubt you, but that still doesn't prove that he didn't try it one time, one night, and he got in over his head. It does happen."

Zeller sighed and nodded, knowing it was true. She didn't think badly of Hall for sounding cynical. She knew it was necessary if they aimed to get to the bottom of this.

"I know," Zeller said. "It does. But it didn't happen to him. I've spoken to both of his roommates, and they've sworn to me that he wasn't doing drugs."

"Or it's a couple of college kids who don't want to admit what they were doing and it got out of hand," Hall said.

"Why can't you just believe her?" Charlotte asked, a little huffy that her boyfriend was being adversarial.

"It's not that I don't want to believe her. But if there was any doubt in the minds of the police, they'd still be investigating."

"The police do make mistakes, you know."

"I know, but just because you think something doesn't make it true. You need some kind of facts or evidence to support the case. If there's a trail to follow, then I'll follow it. But you need to have some bread crumbs to lead the way."

"Olivia, was Keith in trouble in any way that you know of?" Charlotte asked.

"Not that I know of. He was a good-natured person. He didn't try to act like a tough guy, he wasn't into the bar scene, I mean, he wanted to be a biologist. It's not really a career for people who are looking for trouble, is it?"

Hall scoffed. "Take it from me, you don't have to be looking for trouble for it to find you. I've had plenty of experience with that."

"He was a quiet kid. He was in his junior year of college, looking forward to graduating and moving out into the real world."

"Did he ever hang out with any bad kids? Did you know all his friends?"

"I didn't know all his friends, but he never had many. He was always the kind of kid who would have a small group of close friends instead of a ton of casual ones. And I knew most of them. None have ever gotten into trouble that I know of."

"Girlfriends?"

"None right now. He was always kind of awkward talking to girls. He had a girlfriend in high school, and one his freshman year, but nothing in the last year. I think he had a few dates here or there, but no one steady."

"What about work?" Hall asked.

"He worked part time at one of those drugstore-convenience store type places. He stocked shelves, worked a register, things like that."

"How long did he work there?"

"Oh, about a year, I'd say. It's not too far from his apartment, just a block or two. With the campus, everything's pretty close and within walking distance."

"Did he have a car?"

"He had one, but like I said, the college, his apartment, his work, everything was pretty close together. I don't think he used it all that much. If he had to go anywhere, he'd usually walk, ride his bike, or take the bus." Silence filled the air for a minute, as Hall tried to take everything in, and sadness set in for Zeller as she thought of her brother. "Listen, I can tell you're not exactly believing everything yet. Just look around, that's all I ask."

Though she was right, and Hall wasn't buying her story, at least not yet, he could see that the woman was hurting. The sudden loss of someone close to you was never something that was easy to deal with. Some people could cope with it better than others, but it was obvious that Zeller really did believe her brother met death under some mysterious circumstances. Seeing how much she was affected, and because of Charlotte, the least Hall could do was investigate.

"I will look into it," Hall said. "I promise you that."

"Thank you. That's all I can ask."

"I have to ask, though, if I check into this, and I can't find any wrongdoing by anyone, are you going to be OK with that? Can you accept that?"

Zeller let out an anxious kind of smile and shrugged. "Honestly, I don't know. It's just... in my heart, I know something happened. And it wasn't him overdosing on some drug that I know he didn't take."

"If you can write down everything you know about him, addresses, phone numbers, names of friends, co-workers, anyone you think knows him, things like that, it would be really helpful."

"Yeah, I will. Just let me get a notebook."

Zeller got up and left the room, leaving Hall and Charlotte by themselves for a few minutes to discuss everything.

"What do you think?" Charlotte asked.

"I'm not sure you really wanna ask that right now."

"Why not?"

"I don't think you'd like my answer."

Zeller came back into the room and sat down, immediately writing down everything she could think of, which was quite a bit. She and her brother were close, so she knew most of his friends. She also had a surprise for Hall. She removed from her pocket a cell phone and held it up in the air for a second, before handing it over to him.

"What's this?" Hall asked.

"My brother's cell phone. One of his roommates gave it to me."

"Police see this?"

"I don't really know. It was after they concluded their investigation. I'm not sure if they ever looked at it or not. His roommates gave me his stuff, and the phone was amongst the stuff, so I don't know."

"Have you looked through it?"

"Yeah, I did, I didn't notice anything unusual though. But then again, I'm not sure I would notice something even if I saw it. Maybe you'll have better luck with it."

Hall turned it on and made sure there were no codes or passwords that he had to get through. There weren't, and he immediately started looking through it for anything obvious. Nothing jumped out at him at first, but he didn't want to just sit there and look through it in front of Zeller just in case something turned up.

"Can I take this with me?" Hall asked.

"Sure."

Hall put the phone in his pocket and tore out the piece of paper from the notebook that Zeller was writing in. He briefly looked at it to make sure he could read the handwriting, which was no problem, then folded it up and put that in his pocket too.

"Now, about payment, I can probably afford about a thousand dollars," Zeller said. "How much time will that get me? If it takes a while and you find something, I can probably scrape together some more money if you need it."

Hall put his hand up, not really interested in the money. At this point, he was only interested in bringing some kind of closure for Zeller. "It's not about the money."

"No, I don't expect you to work for free. I don't want charity. I intend to pay for your time. If it wasn't you, I'd be paying someone else, so I want you to take it."

"OK. I'll take the money you have. But that's it. If it takes longer, it takes longer. I don't need anything else from you."

Zeller finally let out a normal smile. "It's a deal. So when can you start?"

"I'll start as soon as we leave."

Zeller rubbed her hands together, happy with the answer. "Will you call me with updates?"

Hall grimaced, knowing that was a slippery slope. "I'll let you know what I'm doing or what I'm working on. But I want to be very careful in what I tell you so I don't lead you in one direction, then a few days later, turn around and say the complete opposite. I don't want to get your hopes up."

"Understood."

"OK. So if I tell you I really believe it's looking like one thing or another, it's because I really believe it."

"Thank you."

Zeller went over to Hall and gave him a hug, appreciating that he was looking into the case. She then gave another hug to Charlotte as well, knowing he wouldn't be there without her. Once neither side had any more questions and wrapped everything up, Hall and Charlotte left, ready to embark on their first official case. The pair was quiet as they walked back to the car. Once they reached it, they looked back to the house and waved at Zeller, who was standing by the front door. Before getting in, they stood on opposite sides of the car, talking over the roof of it.

"So what do you think?" Charlotte asked. "And don't give me that I don't wanna know stuff. What do you really think?"

"I dunno. It seems like a stretch to think something happened to the kid. It sounds like a grieving family member who's having trouble processing everything and can't let go."

"She's always been a level-headed person. I don't think that's it."

"Losing someone close to you before it's their time can have a strange effect on people. But, who knows, maybe she's right."

"Really?"

"I mean, all I have to do is go back to my own situation. If I told people that people were after me on a train and thought I was working for some criminal, if I had told them that I was completely innocent, how many people would believe that?"

"I did."

Hall smiled. "You're a special person."

"Thank you for noticing," she replied, though she said it in a way that Hall couldn't quite tell if she was being sarcastic or not.

"Anyway, all I have to do is look at myself as an example to realize that things aren't always what they appear to be. So who knows, maybe we'll find out that she's really onto something."

"Well, whichever way it turns out, thank you."

"Let's save the thanks for if we actually find out anything," he said.

"Even if we don't, and it turns out Keith really did kill himself by overdosing, at least Olivia will have closure. I think that's what she really needs. To know what exactly happened instead of guessing."

"Yeah. I just hope we're able to give that to her."

4

Hall and Charlotte waited until after they had eaten dinner before going down to Keith's apartment to investigate. They didn't know for sure what the roommates' schedules were or if they'd even be home, but they happened to be in luck. Though only one of the roommates was there when Hall and Charlotte knocked, it was better than striking out. Once they knocked on the door, they could hear a TV blaring from inside the apartment. It took a minute for the door to finally open, but once it did, they saw a blond-haired, skinny, twenty-year-old kid standing there with headphones draped around his neck.

"Help ya?"

Hall briefly looked at Charlotte before answering. "Yeah, we're private—well, Olivia Zeller hired us to look into the death of her brother, and we just wanted to talk to you, ask you a few questions if you don't mind."

"Yeah, sure, come on in."

Hall and Charlotte walked in, observing an apartment that looked like it hadn't been cleaned in a while. There was dust on the tables, dirt on the floor, magazines, papers, and games spread across a wooden rectangular coffee table. If they'd have gone into the kitchen, they would have found dirty dishes in the sink and pots and pans all over the countertops.

"Sorry about the mess and all. Cleaning's not really high on my priority list these days."

Hall laughed. "No, I get it, no big deal."

"So what do you guys wanna know?"

"Which roommate are you?"

"Oh, I'm Anderson."

"Anderson?"

"Yeah, it's my first name, weird I know. Every time I tell people, they assume I'm just giving them my last name or I'm holding back my name or something."

"Well, to start with, what do you think about everything that happened?" Hall asked.

"It's crazy, man, like, I still can't believe it. I just... I just don't get it. I don't understand what happened."

"Who found his body?"

"We did. Me and my other roommate, that is, Brian."

"What time was that?"

"Probably around eleven or so."

"Did you know he was dead right away?"

"Yeah, pretty much. We checked his pulse, didn't have any. Brian knows CPR, so he tried to revive him, but it didn't do any good. I called an ambulance and the cops, but by the time they got here, there was nothing they could do. He was already gone."

"And the police thought it was an overdose?" Charlotte asked.

Anderson shrugged. "That's what they said."

Hall could tell by the kid's mannerisms that he didn't believe it. "But you don't think so?"

"I mean, I told the police that Keith didn't do drugs or anything, but they didn't listen to us. They had their evidence, or whatever, so that's all they needed, I guess."

"He didn't do drugs? You sure of that?"

Anderson looked to the floor and rubbed around his mouth, like he had something on his mind that he wasn't sharing. Hall knew that asking questions like this sometimes made people clam up, not wanting to make anyone sound bad, or hide something that they were doing themselves. It was something they'd have to get past if they wanted the truth.

"Listen," Hall said. "Whatever you guys did or didn't do, it stays in this room. If there's anything illegal going on, I'm not gonna report it to the police or anything; you're not gonna get in trouble. I'm just here to find out what happened."

Anderson cleared his throat. "Well, I mean, he

smoked a joint every now and then, but that's about it. He didn't do any hard stuff."

"You're positive?"

"Yeah, I am. I've roomed with him for three years. Well, this is our third year. We met at freshmen orientation and have been friends ever since. I know for a fact he never did any of that stuff."

"How do you know?"

"Umm... because I have occasionally... dabbled in some stuff. And every time I asked him if he wanted to do it too, he always turned it down. Always. And I knew he would, but, you know, it's always nice to ask just in case someone changes their mind or something."

"Maybe he decided to do it by himself, without other people looking at him or judging him?"

Anderson shook his head. "Nah, not him."

"Why not?" Charlotte asked.

"Because he wouldn't even do pot by himself. We had plenty of conversations about this stuff. I mean, he always felt that if it was a party, or a group of people, yeah, he might smoke a joint or two or something, but that was it. Once the party was over, once the people were gone, he felt like he had to go back to being Mr. Responsible." Anderson then let out a laugh, thinking about his friend. "In fact, that's what we called him sometimes. Mr. Responsible. Because you always knew he was going to try to do the right thing. He'd stay out of trouble. You could always count on that."

"What kind of evidence did the police have?" Hall asked.

"Well, there was a new hole in his arm and a needle on the floor next to his body. That's all the evidence they needed."

"You ever see him with a needle before?"

"Nope."

"So you don't think he did this to himself?"

"No, I don't."

The three of them were quiet for a few seconds as Hall thought of another question. Charlotte beat him to it though.

"If you don't think he did it to himself, then someone had to do it for him," Charlotte said. "Isn't that right?"

"I mean, I guess. I don't know. I just know Keith wouldn't have put that needle in his own arm. I mean, I know it. And I don't have any proof to say he didn't." Anderson then patted his chest over his heart. "I just know it in here."

"If that's the case, then someone murdered him," Hall said.

"I mean, I don't know, I guess if that's what it comes down to."

"Who would wanna do that?"

"Nobody I know."

"He have trouble with anyone?"

"He never mentioned it," Anderson answered.

"Did his behavior change recently? Like, more

reserved, get angry over small things, anything like that?"

Anderson thought for a few seconds, but nothing came to him. "No, he acted the same as always. He was a pretty upbeat guy for the most part. Liked to joke around. Just the day before his death, we were joking around, playing Xbox, just like normal."

"What about Brian, your other roommate?" Charlotte asked.

"What about him?"

"Him and Keith get along?"

"Oh, yeah, they didn't have any problems."

"How long have they known each other?"

"About the same as me. We were all in some of the same classes together as freshmen. Me and Keith got an apartment midway through the year, then last year, we asked Brian to split it with us. Believe me, if you think Brian had something to do with it, you're off base. They were tight."

"Well, one thing's for sure, isn't it?" Hall asked.

"What's that?"

"If Keith didn't put that needle in his arm himself, then someone did it for him. Isn't that right?"

Anderson nodded. "Yeah."

"What about work? Any issues there?"

"Not that I know of. It's a small, family-type pharmacy around the corner from here."

"He like it there?"

"I guess. Never really complained about it. I mean,

there were the days every now and then when he didn't feel like going in, but that's pretty much everybody from time to time, isn't it?"

"Yeah. How about other kids in school? Problems with anyone?"

"No, he didn't really interact with too many other students, unless there was a party or something. He wasn't a real big social guy. I mean, he could blend in fine once the party got started, but nobody would ever confuse him as being the life of it."

"What about girls?" Charlotte asked. "Did he have his eye on anyone? Maybe fighting with another guy over someone?"

Anderson shook his head. "No. I mean, there were some girls in his classes that he was interested in, but he never took the plunge as far as actually asking any of them out or anything. He was kinda shy around girls."

"Maybe one of them had a boyfriend who thought otherwise?"

"Nah, he definitely wasn't the type who'd go fighting to the death over someone. If he was gonna go out with a girl, she'd probably have to ask him out. He just got really nervous and tense around the opposite sex, you know, wasn't sure what to say, how to act, things like that."

"What about a dark secret?" Hall asked. "Could he have been hiding one?"

"Like what?"

"I don't know, you tell me. You're saying he didn't do drugs, didn't have issues with anyone, had no problems in his life, yet here he was found dead with a needle in his arm. How do you explain that?"

Anderson shrugged. "I can't."

"Think we could see his room?"

"Yeah. There's not really much left that's his though. We gave most of it back to his sister and all."

"Never know."

Anderson led the pair into the bedroom that he and Keith shared. Since it was a two-bedroom apartment, they shared one room, while Brian took the other. It was as messy as the rest of the house. The bed wasn't made, there were clothes all over the floor, and there was a desk that had junk all over it. Hall went over to Keith's bed, turning it over, looking under it, even running his hands along the mattress to see if there was a secret compartment that Keith might have hid something in. After turning up nothing, Hall went to the desk and ruffled through things, with Anderson's permission, but still came up empty. Charlotte checked the bathroom as Hall went through the closet, both of them finding nothing of interest.

"Anything?" Hall asked.

"Nothing," Charlotte replied.

"We should've checked through the things that Olivia had before we left to see if there was anything here."

"Well, she already went through everything. I'm

sure if anything weird was in there she would have told us."

"Yeah, probably."

The three of them left the bedroom and went back into the living room to finish their conversation.

"So what's your theory?" Hall asked.

"I don't have one," Anderson answered.

"You don't even have a guess?"

"No."

"Listen, this thing went down one of two ways. One, he overdosed and killed himself. Two, someone did it for him. Which is it?"

"I don't know. I'm telling you, I don't know. All I know is that Keith wouldn't have done that to himself."

"So someone killed him?"

"I don't know what happened. But I'm a hundred percent sure what didn't happen."

Hall and Charlotte looked at each other, both seeming to have run out of questions for the kid.

"Look, why don't you talk to Brian? I mean, we've already gone over this countless times in the last couple weeks since it happened, and neither of us have been able to make much sense of it. But maybe he'll remember something if you guys talk to him. Maybe he can give you something."

"Well, one thing's for sure, isn't it?" Hall said. "Somebody's gotta know something."

5

Anderson said that Brian was at his job, so Hall and Charlotte went over to the pizza shop where Brian worked. Being on campus, it was a popular hangout with most of the kids, and it always seemed busy. When they got there, there were only a few tables open. Charlotte grabbed one of them near the back as Hall went up to the counter. A thin middle-aged man came over to check on him.

"How's it going? What can I help you with?"

"Information," Hall answered. "Can I speak with the manager?"

"That's me. Owner, manager, and everything in between."

"Oh, OK. I'm investigating the death of Keith Zeller, and I need to talk to his roommate Brian. I understand he works here."

"Yeah, Brian works here. Real shame about what happened."

"Did Keith ever come in here?"

"Yeah, sure did, bunch of times. Even when Brian wasn't working, he and Keith would come in, have a slice, sometimes with their other buddy, too. What's his name... Anderson. Yeah, a lot of times the three of them would come in, hang out."

"They ever get in any trouble or anything?"

"Them? Nah. Good bunch of boys. Never any problems. Respectful of others, courteous, manners; don't find kids like that all the time these days."

"Brian ever mention any worries about Keith or anything?"

"Not to me. Just out of curiosity, what's to investigate? Didn't the kid overdose or something?"

"That's the official word," Hall said.

"You don't buy it?"

"Let's just say I have some doubts. While the kids were in here, did you ever see them engaged in any heated discussions, looking worried, anything like that?"

The man looked away for a second at a pizza box that was next to him on the counter, trying to remember all the times the kids were in there. "No, I don't remember anything if there was. But like I said, they're a good bunch of kids."

"Well, thanks for your time."

"Yeah, no problem. Hey, wait a minute. I just

thought of something."

"What?" Hall asked.

"Couple weeks ago, Keith came in here by himself. I remember thinking it was pretty strange that he was in here alone."

"Why? Didn't happen often?"

"Never happened at all. He was never in here by himself. Always with Brian and Anderson. At least one of them."

"How soon was this before he died?"

"Oh, I'd say a few days, maybe a week."

"What was he doing?" Hall asked. "He have anything with him? Books, papers, anything?"

"No, was just sitting there eating a slice, having a soda. Looked like he was preoccupied or something. Was just kind of staring. Didn't seem like he was with it. You know how it is when you got something on your mind, you just kind of blank out?"

"Yeah. And nobody ever joined him?"

"Not that I saw. Brian wasn't even working that night."

"How long was he here for?"

"I don't know, I'd say half hour, forty-five minutes. Maybe even an hour, I'm not sure. I just remember thinking it was so weird to see him here all alone without his buddies."

"You think I could talk to Brian for a few minutes?" Hall asked. "I know you're busy, so I won't take up too much of his time, just five minutes maybe?"

"Yeah, sure, take all the time you need. I got plenty of help tonight. Since you're here, you wanna order something?"

Hall grinned. "Yeah, OK. I'll take two slices of pepperoni and two Cokes."

"You got it, my man, two slices coming up."

Hall took out some money to pay for it, but the owner quickly stopped him. "This one's on me, my friend."

"No, that's OK."

"No, really," the owner insisted. "It's on me. You really wanna pay me for these? You find out what really happened to that kid."

Hall nodded. "I will."

"Take a seat and I'll bring it right over to you."

"Me and my girlfriend are seated right back there," Hall said, pointing to the table Charlotte had taken.

"I'll send Brian over with it."

"Thank you."

Hall went over to their table and sat down next to Charlotte. As they waited for Brian and their food, he gave her a rundown of what the owner had told him.

"That's a pretty big coincidence, don't you think?" Charlotte asked. "I mean, he does something unusual, something he never does, then he winds up dead a week later?"

"Showing up at a pizza shop by yourself isn't really evidence that something happened."

"But it does make you think a little harder."

"I guess it does do that."

"Admit it, after talking to Anderson, and this piece of news, you're not as certain about him overdosing, are you?"

"I'm not ready to leap to any other conclusions at the moment," Hall said.

"You're stubborn, do you know that?"

"Yes, I know."

"Why won't you at least consider it?"

"I am considering it. I've changed my stance somewhat."

"You have?" Charlotte asked. "To what?"

"Well, at the beginning I was ninety percent sure that Keith overdosed on his own. Now, I'm only seventy-five percent sure. See? I'm changing."

Charlotte didn't seem all that impressed with his new stance. "Wow. Big change."

A few minutes later, an average looking kid with shoulder length black hair came over to the table, handing the pizza to the guests. Brian was pretty average in every respect. Average looks, average height, average weight, everything about him was pretty average except for one thing: he was a pretty mean guitar player. Music was really what he was passionate about. He was in a small band and hoped to do something music related once he was done school. He'd been playing guitar since he was six, and, if Brian's band didn't make it big—or at least enough to make a living with it, he hoped to still stay connected somehow. Whether it was teaching others, or working in the industry, music was his thing.

"You guys the PIs?"

"We look the part that much, huh?" Hall asked.

"Well, you kinda look like a cop with the haircut, but they said you didn't show a badge or anything."

"Maybe you got a future in the business."

Brian smiled, sitting down across from them. "Not me, man, I got other plans."

"Like what? What do you plan on doing when you're done school?"

"I dunno. Hopefully I can make a living with my music. We'll see how that goes."

"What do you play?"

"Mostly guitar. Sing a little bit."

"You good?"

"Well, I don't like to brag too much, but yeah, I'm not too bad."

"Well, I guess you know we're here about Keith," Hall said.

A sad look came over Brian's face. "Yeah."

"What can you tell us about him?"

"He was a good dude. Happy guy for the most part. Kept to himself. Not really a partier or anything."

"Drugs?"

"Not that I ever saw. I think he smoked a joint, like, once a month, something like that. Certainly wasn't someone who was hooked on it or anything."

"Hard stuff?"

Brian shook his head. "No, drugs weren't his thing."

"Except when he was found dead with a needle in his arm."

"Yeah, I guess. I don't know what happened there, but it's hard to believe."

"What, you think someone killed him?"

"What? No. Who'd wanna hurt Keith?"

"I don't know, that's what I'm trying to find out."

"I can't imagine he's had too many enemies in his life who would wanna do that."

"Everyone tells me Keith was a good kid who didn't do drugs, but there he was."

Brian looked down at the table, still shaking his head, trying to make some kind of sense out of everything. "Yeah, I guess he did the one time, right? The facts are the facts. No matter how many times we say he didn't do it, I guess he had to, huh?"

"What if he didn't?" Charlotte asked. "What if someone killed him and made it look like he overdosed?"

Brian looked at her like she was crazy. "Who'd wanna do that?"

"That's what we're trying to find out."

Brian lifted his hand up, then slapped it back down on the table. "I guess it's possible, but like I said, I don't know of anyone who had a problem with Keith."

"What about you and Anderson?" Hall asked.

"What about us?"

"Either of you two have problems with him from time to time?"

"What? No. That's crazy. If you're thinking one of us set him up or something, that's just way out there."

"You always look to the people who are the closest to the victim. And that would be you guys."

"Nooo... no way. Listen, if I had a problem with him, I'd just move out and find another place. I certainly wouldn't kill him. I couldn't kill anybody."

"What about Anderson?"

"Anderson? Are you kidding? Anderson's a good friend of mine, but have you seen the guy? I doubt he could snap a pencil in half, let alone kill someone."

"Well, Keith's sister doesn't believe he killed himself, and if she's right, someone had it in for him," Charlotte said.

"I've met his sister, and she's really cool and all, but I think she just doesn't wanna admit that Keith tried something he shouldn't have, and he got in over his head."

"And that's what you believe?" Hall asked.

"I guess so. It's what the cops said."

"Your boss told us Keith was in here last week by himself, which was unusual, and that he looked like he had something on his mind. You know anything about that?"

"First I've heard of it."

"Keith didn't mention it?"

"No."

"In the week or two before his death, did Keith seem different? Like he had something on his mind? Something he was hiding? Stressed? Anything like that?"

Brian thought for a few seconds, but couldn't come up with anything at first. "No, I can't think of anything. Seemed the same as always."

"Nothing?" Charlotte asked, believing someone had to notice some type of sign if he was in trouble.

Brian shook his head, trying to think of something, though nothing was coming to him. "Nothing that I can think of."

"Well, I guess…"

"Wait a minute," Brian said, suddenly remembering something, though he didn't know if it was important or connected at all.

"You got something?" Hall asked.

"Maybe. It was like, two or three days before Keith died. It was around ten, maybe eleven, and we'd both just gotten home from work. Anderson wasn't there. I think he was at a party or something. But Keith got home first, and I don't know how long he was there, but he seemed kind of depressed about something."

"Do you know what?"

"No, he didn't say. He was at the kitchen table with a book open, so I just assumed he was having a problem with one of his classes."

"You ask about it?"

"Yeah, 'cause I came home and started talking to

him, but he wasn't talking back. He looked like he was in some kind of zone or something. I asked if he needed help with anything and he said no, that he could handle it."

"Those were his words? I can handle it?"

"Yeah, that's what he said exactly."

"And that was it?"

"Yeah. I figured he was upset and didn't want to talk about it so I went in my room and watched TV."

"You think it could've been something other than school related?" Charlotte asked.

"Who knows? I mean, maybe."

"Did you ever notice him like that before?" Hall asked. "With anything, whether it was school, work, personal?"

"No, not really," Brian answered. "I mean, Keith was pretty smart. He usually didn't need help with school. He was the one who was usually helping us with things."

"He ever express any frustration with his job?"

"Not really. Now that I think of it, though, it did seem like he didn't like it as much lately."

"How's that?"

"Well, he always enjoyed going. I think he started working there last year, maybe the year before, anyway, he never complained about going in. Sometimes he'd pick up an extra shift here or there. Not like some guys who don't wanna work. He wanted to go, pick up extra money."

"And that changed?"

"Yeah. I'd say the last few weeks," Brian replied. "It was almost like he had to drag himself in, you know?"

"What gave you that impression?"

"Well, before, whenever he had work, he was still upbeat, smiling, joking around, he was still in a good mood. But the last few weeks, whenever he had work, it seemed like he was mad or something. He never seemed excited about going in or anything."

"He say why?"

"No, never talked about it. I just figured it was a guy who was getting tired of being there. Figured he'd be looking for a new job soon. I mean, most people get bored with a job after a while, right? I just assumed that's what was happening with him."

They talked for a few more minutes, though Hall and Charlotte didn't learn anything else that would be considered important.

"You guys really think something happened to him?" Brian asked.

"I don't know," Hall answered. "That's what we're trying to find out. When everyone says he didn't do something, and that's how he died, it makes you wonder, doesn't it?"

Brian nodded. "Yeah."

"What do you think?"

"I just assumed it was like the cops said, but..."

"But what?"

"Who knows? It's hard to believe he did that to

himself."

"One last question before we go."

"OK?"

"Were you the first one to find him when he died?" Hall asked.

"No, I think Anderson was. I mean, we were both out together, and got back at the same time, but he walked in first, I think. Why?"

"Well, doesn't really matter. I was just wondering if you noticed anything unusual? A mark on the door, an extra drink on a table, something on the floor, something out of place or not where it usually was, anything like that?"

Brian scratched his chin as he thought about it. He still remembered the night vividly. Seeing his friend lying on the floor wasn't something a person easily forgot. "No, I don't think so. But I can't really say for sure. As soon as I got in and Anderson said something, I pretty much started CPR immediately. I didn't really notice much else. Then, afterwards, I think we were in too much shock to really think about anything else."

"Keith have any other friends who might know anything you think?"

"He had other friends, but nobody who knew him as well as me and Anderson did. We were the closest to him. Never know, I guess."

"All right, that's all we got," Hall said. "Thanks for the help."

"No problem." Brian stood up, though he didn't

leave yet, and stood at the edge of the table. "If this turns out to be something else, that someone did this to Keith, will you let me know?"

"We can do that."

"Thanks." Brian nodded and smiled before leaving.

"You thinking what I'm thinking?" Charlotte asked.

"Probably," Hall replied. "What are you thinking?"

"That maybe he had something going on at work. Maybe he was having trouble with a co-worker or something."

"Could be."

"So are we going there next?"

Hall looked at the time. "Let's make it in the morning."

"Why?"

"Because we have this pizza to finish first and it's getting late. His workplace will still be there tomorrow."

"I guess. I'd rather do it now, though."

"We're gonna do some research on that place first."

"What research?" Charlotte asked.

"Well, you're the computer expert. You're gonna find out as much as you can about this little pharmacy. See if there's ever been any problems there before."

"Oh. Good idea."

"That way if there is, we're already armed with that knowledge going in."

"Good thinking."

"I try."

6

The next morning, by the time Hall came over to Charlotte's apartment, ready to go to the pharmacy that Keith worked at, she was already armed with information. She dug into all the records she could find and used the hacking skills she learned from her former boyfriend to get the ones that weren't so easily found. In essence, she found nothing. She couldn't find any complaints, any issues, any police trouble, nothing out of the ordinary. It wasn't what she wanted to find, or what Hall was hoping for. They were hoping they would find a host of issues, leading them to conclude that it was a hostile work environment, and, therefore, making it more likely that someone had done Keith in. But the evidence didn't suggest that was likely.

Hall walked in, seeing Charlotte hard at work on her laptop at the kitchen table. She only briefly acknowledged his presence, not wanting to break her concentration. Hall walked over to her, and after giving her a kiss, he sat next to her.

"So whatcha got?"

Charlotte stopped typing and turned her head toward him, giving him a pouty face. She shook her head and sighed. "Nothing."

"Nothing?"

"Nothing."

"You can't find anything?"

"Oh, I found lots of stuff," Charlotte answered. "But nothing to suggest there's something funny going on there."

Hall still couldn't believe it. "Nothing?"

"Bob's Family Pharmacy has been open about fifteen years. They sponsor local little league teams, help the homeless, donate to children's charities, and seem like a pillar of the community. If you look at their reviews on various online sites, you'll see hundreds with an average rating of four point eight out of five, all praising how much they love the place. I've found no police issues, no complaints, nothing to suggest they are anything but a great place to work or shop."

"Almost sounds too good to be true."

"Well, these smaller businesses, at least the well-run ones, tend to get better ratings than bigger businesses. They cater to customers more, they're more invested in the business so they're more interested in making customers happy and wanting them to return."

"Yeah, I know. I was just hoping to find something unusual. If there wasn't anything in Keith's personal life that caused him problems, then it had to be there."

"I know, but I can't find anything."

"Maybe there's nothing to be found," Hall said. "Maybe we just have to see for ourselves. Maybe someone says something that sounds weird." Charlotte huffed, and Hall could tell something else was on her mind. "What's the matter?"

"It's just... all this time I've assumed—I've been so sure like Olivia said—that Keith wasn't the type of kid who would do that to himself. But the more we're looking into it, it's not looking like anyone else would've done it either. Maybe we're just wrong."

"That's why I told you to reserve judgment until you see the facts. Family members can be blinded, and it's totally understandable that they would, but they don't want to see that someone close to them, someone they've known a long time, has a darker side that they didn't know about or didn't recognize. It's just hard to cope with."

"It's gonna be so hard for Olivia to deal with that."

"Well, let's not get all doom and gloom already," Hall said. "We're not done yet. We still have his work, and who knows, maybe that will lead to something else."

"I know you don't really believe that."

"It doesn't really matter what either one of us believes. The only thing that matters is what we can prove, and that there are more doors left to open. No need to assume anything until all those doors are bolted shut."

Hall and Charlotte then ate breakfast together, having something light to get them going. Then they went down to the campus, where the pharmacy was located. It opened at nine o'clock, and they wanted to get there as early as possible. The pharmacy was located at the corner of an intersection on a busy street, and though there was only street parking out front, there was a small parking lot in the rear of the building.

Hall and Charlotte arrived at the pharmacy about twenty minutes after it opened. Before going inside the store, they walked around the area for a few minutes, trying to get a feel for the neighborhood. They walked up and down the street, seeing kids with backpacks speeding past them, people walking their dogs, businessmen and women with laptop bags and briefcases. Stores and businesses were well kept. There wasn't graffiti on walls or trash on the ground. There was nothing to suggest it was a sketchy area. Of course, it was bright and early. They knew a lot of times, no matter how nice an area was, it was the cover of night that brought out the criminal element.

Once Hall and Charlotte went inside, they were immediately greeted by an employee working the front counter.

"Hello, how you guys doing?" the woman asked politely.

"Good," Hall replied.

Hall and Charlotte kept walking and went down a few aisles.

"Aren't we gonna talk to someone?" Charlotte asked.

"Yeah. Figured we'd just walk around for a bit, kind of take everything in. See if anything interesting pops up."

"What interesting thing could pop up at ten in the morning?"

Hall looked at her. "Point taken."

They went back up to the front counter and asked to see the manager. They only had to wait a minute or two until they saw a middle-aged woman coming towards them.

"Hi, my name's Sharon. Can I help you?"

"Are you the manager?" Charlotte asked.

"Yes. Is there a problem?"

"No, no problem," Hall replied. "My name's Brandon, this is Charlotte. We're investigating the death of Keith Zeller."

"Keith... such a tragedy. It's hard not seeing his face around here anymore."

"I'm sure it's been hard. What can you tell us about him?"

"I'm sorry, are you police officers?"

"No, we're private investigators," Charlotte answered.

The manager stared at the two of them, looking somewhat distrustful of the pair. Hall noticed she suddenly seemed uneasy. Her stance changed, she folded her arms, and her body language indicated that she wasn't pleased to see them. But that was just his first impression.

"Oh, I see," Sharon said. "Private investigators. OK. What would private investigators be looking into his death for? Didn't he overdose?"

"Seems to be the prevailing opinion," Hall answered.

"But you don't think so?"

"It's not what we think, it's what we can prove."

"His sister seems to think that someone killed him," Charlotte said, drawing a look from Hall, who didn't seem pleased that she mentioned it.

"Ah, well, you can kind of understand her not wanting to accept the truth."

"So you think he did it?" Hall asked, a little surprised that she seemed so willing to jump to that conclusion.

Sharon smiled. "Like you said, it's not what I think, it's what's been proven. The police have already ruled it that way, haven't they? If there was evidence to the contrary, I'm sure they would have kept the case open, would they not?"

"The police do make mistakes you know."

"I wouldn't know. I wasn't there. All I can do is rely on what I've been told. Police said it was an overdose, I have to take them at their word."

"It's kind of weird that you're so willing to take them at their word when nobody else does," Charlotte said. "Keith's sister, both his roommates, all say that he didn't use drugs. They say he wouldn't have done that."

"We all know that some people will deny anything because they don't want to believe it. That doesn't make it true."

"Did you have any problems with Keith here?" Hall asked.

"Not at all. He was a good employee. Always showed up and did his job."

"Forgive me for saying this, but I'm sensing some hostility."

"It's just that I've already spoken to the police about this. I thought it was closed. Everybody who's known Keith has already had a hard-enough time with this. You guys coming in, asking questions, poking around, is only going to prolong the torture for everyone. It's tough to find closure if you're going to keep asking everyone questions about it."

"Well, we're going to keep asking them until we find out the truth," Charlotte said.

"The truth is that Keith tried something and overdosed. It happens. He wouldn't be the first person to do that, and I'm sure he won't be the last. It's reality. Refusing to accept that belief will only keep everyone who knows him living in the past. It's not healthy for anyone."

"You really believe that?"

"Until someone shows me proof that he didn't overdose... yes."

"Did Keith ever have any trouble or problems with anyone here? Other employees, customers, anything?"

"Not to my knowledge," Sharon replied. "Everyone here seemed to like him. And he was always good with customers. No problems."

"We heard that Keith's behavior changed a little the last few weeks," Hall said. "You know anything about that?"

"Changed how?"

"For one, he didn't seem as enthusiastic about coming here. One night after work, one of his roommates came home and found him depressed after working that night. Another time he was seen all alone in a pizza shop, which was very unusual for him."

"Everyone has a bad day at work," Sharon said. "That's not that unusual. And as for being alone in a pizza shop, I mean, everyone likes to be alone every now and then."

"So you don't put stock into any of that?"

"It sounds to me like you're grasping at straws."

"You don't think there's any chance of some kind of foul play at all?"

"Not really, no. Look, Keith was a good kid. I liked him. But it's time for everyone to accept the truth, to live in reality, and accept the fact that he's gone. Refusing to admit that isn't doing anyone any good."

"You're the manager, right?" Charlotte asked. "Is there any chance we could talk to the owners?"

"What for?"

Charlotte shrugged. "Maybe they'll say something different."

"They won't."

"But how do you know?"

"Because they'd only met Keith a couple times. They're basically absentee owners. They're about seventy years old; they don't want anything to do with running the business day-to-day. They come in once every couple of weeks to check on everything, talk with me, then they're gone."

"So you basically run everything?" Hall asked.

"That's right."

"Who else here was tight with Keith?"

"I don't know. No one really."

"You mean he's worked here for two years and he wasn't close to anyone?"

"People who work together don't have to be friends, you know. He was friendly with everyone, but I don't think he was especially close with anyone as far as hanging out after work or anything."

"So there's no one else we can talk to about him?"

Sharon shook her head. "Not that I know of."

Hall and Charlotte could see that they weren't going to get anything else out of the manager. She was starting to repeat the same answers over and over again. Hall looked at Charlotte to see if she was done with the questions, which she was.

"OK, well, we've taken up enough of your time, so we'll get out of your hair now," Hall said.

"No problem," Sharon replied.

"Would you like us to be in touch with you again?"

"For what?"

"Well, we're gonna keep digging into this until we find something, and I have a feeling we will. Just wondering if you'd wanna be kept up to date when we do."

"You're really going to keep on going with this?"

"Any reason why we shouldn't?"

"You really think something criminal happened to him?"

"I do. And I'm gonna keep after it until I can prove it."

7

Charlotte and Hall had been driving for several minutes after leaving the pharmacy. They'd both been quiet. They were both thinking about the case, and especially what Sharon had told them.

"What are you thinking right now?" Charlotte asked.

"I'm thinking that didn't go exactly like I thought it would."

"How so?"

"She was a little more defiant than I assumed she would be."

"You think she's hiding something?"

"Not necessarily," Hall replied. "It could be she just really thinks it's all a waste of time."

"Don't you think it's a little strange that she says

nobody else there knows him that well? He worked there for two years."

"Just 'cause you work with people doesn't mean you get all chummy with them though. Especially people who are more reserved."

"I think it's weird that everyone we talked to so far was insistent that Keith didn't do drugs and wouldn't have done this to himself. But this woman accepts it at the drop of a hat."

"Could be that she didn't know him as well. You know, just because you work with someone, doesn't mean you know what they're really like, especially when they're not in a work setting. Especially if you're a boss. I think it's very rare that a boss would get close enough to an employee to know what they're really like in another place."

"There was just something about her. She didn't even seem like she wanted to entertain the thought that something else happened."

"I dunno. Could be a lot of things."

"So where are we going now?" Charlotte asked.

Hall hesitated for a second, still thinking about it himself. "Let's go to the police station."

"What? Why?"

"Maybe they can give us more details."

Charlotte agreed, and they headed over to the station, and immediately, upon entering, noticed that it was a bit busy. Looked to be a line of about six people ahead of them at the front desk.

"Are you sure this is a good idea?" Charlotte asked.

"Why not?"

"Because I'm not so sure they'll be eager to talk to you about this."

Hall shrugged. "Worst they can do is say no. Besides, I think I still have some cred because of the Palumbo thing."

"That was over two months ago. How long do you think they'll keep that in their memory banks?"

"Hopefully long enough."

After ten minutes of waiting, it was finally their turn to talk to the desk officer.

"Can I help you?" the officer asked.

"Yeah, I was wondering if I could talk to Detective Bradham?"

"He expecting you?"

"Not exactly. But it is about a case."

"Hold on."

The officer picked up the phone and called Bradham's office. The detective answered and said he'd be down right away.

"Have a seat," the officer said. "He'll be here in a minute."

"Thanks a lot."

Hall and Charlotte went over to the chairs to sit down, but didn't even get the chance to sit before they saw Bradham walking out. Hall and Charlotte walked up to him.

"Hey," Bradham said. "You the people waiting for me?"

"Sure are," Hall replied.

"Nice to see you guys again. You know you were such a big help on that Palumbo thing. Couldn't have done it without you."

A strange look came over Hall's face, temporarily forgetting their current issue. "What was there to do? They all killed each other before you even got there."

"Like I said, couldn't have done it without you," Bradham said with a smile. "So what's up? Something about a case we're working on?"

Hall looked around. "Yeah. Could we talk somewhere more privately?"

"Sure. Let's go to my office."

They went to Bradham's office and closed the door so the detective could listen to the pair without being bothered.

"So, what's going on?" Bradham asked.

"Do you know anything about the Keith Zeller case?"

Bradham briefly looked away and scratched his nose as he thought about the name. "Doesn't ring a bell. Who is he?"

"Well, about two weeks ago he showed up as a dead body," Hall said.

"And? You know something about it?"

"I'd like to know more about it to be honest."

"Why, what's your connection?"

Hall cleared his throat, knowing this probably wasn't going to come out like he wanted it to. "Well, Zeller's sister hired us to look into it. I guess it was listed as a suicide or an overdose, and she believes that's not the case. She thinks someone killed him."

Bradham put his hand up, not wanting to hear anything else about it at the moment. "What do you mean she hired you?"

Hall shrugged. "Just what I said. She's paying us to look into it."

"Why? You're not investigators."

"Well…"

"We've started our own private investigation company," Charlotte said, answering for her partner.

"You have?"

"Yes."

"You got a license?"

"Well…"

Hall was interrupted again by his girlfriend. "You don't need a license to investigate something. Only if you intend to advertise your services. Right now, we're not. At least until we get it."

"Is that right?" Bradham said. "You guys got a license to carry?"

Hall looked at Charlotte before answering, making sure he could get a turn. "Neither one of us is carrying a gun."

"Oh. Well, what are you looking into this for?

How'd this woman hook up with you two if you're not advertising your services?"

"She's a friend of mine," Charlotte answered. "I used to work with her."

"Oh. How lucky for her."

"Isn't it?" Charlotte said with a smile.

Bradham brought up Zeller's file on his computer and started reading it. "What is it that you're trying to do?"

"Figure out if someone killed him or not," Hall replied.

"Looks like a pretty open and shut case. Overdosed on heroin."

"Except everyone who knows him says he didn't do that."

Bradham rolled his eyes. "It's the same old story. You know how many criminals go to jail kicking and screaming that they didn't do it? All of them. And it doesn't matter how much evidence you have to the contrary. They still swear it wasn't them."

"So you didn't investigate this?"

"I did not, no. Detective Shore was the investigating officer on this. So this guy's sister says he was killed? She have evidence to support that?"

"No."

"She have anything?"

"She just knows her brother didn't do drugs," Charlotte said.

Bradham had a cynical look in his eyes that had

been colored by ten years of investigations in the detective division. "So you're investigating this based on what? Which way the wind blows?"

"Can you tell us any specifics about the crime scene?" Hall asked.

Bradham stared at the screen. "Looks like there's not much to tell. He was found in the middle of the room, needle mark in his arm, heroin next to his body. Autopsy confirmed the heroin in his system, which looks like it'd been enough to stop a rhinoceros."

"Anything strange or unusual?"

"Not really. No signs of forced entry. Everything in the room was intact, no mess, no signs of a struggle, nothing missing. No reason to go any further."

"No other needle marks in his arm other than the one?"

Bradham read through the file. "That's correct."

"Don't you think it's strange? How many people on heroin only have one mark on their arm?"

"Gotta start somewhere."

"And it just so happens that it's the one that kills him? And why would he do so much? Don't you think he'd start with a smaller dosage just to see what it's like first?"

"I don't know what the kid was thinking," Bradham said. "Could be any number of different things."

"Could be someone had a problem with him and shoved that needle in his arm," Charlotte said.

"There's no evidence of that. If that were the case,

don't you think there'd be evidence of a struggle? A lamp knocked over, papers on the ground, things like that? I mean, if I wanna stick a needle in your arm, and you know you're in trouble, you're not just gonna stand there and let me do it, right? You're gonna fight and kick and scream, are you not?"

"I guess so."

"Autopsy didn't pick up anything else that might indicate something was done to him?" Hall asked.

Bradham read the report. "Not a thing. Thinking maybe he was drugged or something first that would make him so out of it you could shove a horse up his ass and he wouldn't notice?"

"Something like that."

"Sorry to disappoint you."

"Guess we'll just have to keep on digging."

"Let me ask you something. Why do you really think someone killed this guy? Just because his sister says so? Because let me tell you, in my experience, and I've seen this a lot, when there's someone who's in trouble, whether it's drugs, or anything else, their family members are usually the last ones to know."

"I realize that."

"Because if it's one thing these people don't want to do, it's disappoint their family, their friends, by letting them think they're doing something they shouldn't."

"I don't know," Hall said. "I was initially skeptical myself. But now…"

"Well, what evidence have you uncovered to change that view?"

"Nothing concrete. Just a feeling."

"We can't operate on feelings. We need proof."

"I know. It just seems strange to me that a kid who has no history, whose family and friends swear he wouldn't have done what it looks like he did, all of a sudden overdoses."

"I can tell you haven't investigated this kind of stuff before," Bradham said.

"Why?"

"Because it happens. Kids—and even adults—don't know what they're doing; they think they're gonna get some big high, and they shoot themselves up with way too much, and they wind up dead. It happens. Unfortunate, yes, but it still happens. And it happens to addicts who've been shooting up for years, and it happens to people who are doing it for the first time. As unfortunate as it is, there's nothing to suggest any kind of criminal behavior is linked to this kid."

"Did you guys talk to his friends, roommates, co-workers?"

"Yeah, looks like it. Nothing unusual to report there."

"Well, we talked to them too," Charlotte said. "And it looks like there might have been something going on at work."

"Such as?"

"We don't know yet. But he seemed to be acting

differently the last week or so he was alive. Didn't want to go to work, seemed to have something on his mind, going off alone, things like that."

Bradham was still unconvinced. "Could've been anything. Maybe he was thinking about quitting. People do it all the time, you know. Some people get hung up over things like that. It's a life change. Not sure if you're doing the right thing, what if it doesn't work out, all those things."

Hall didn't think that was it. "This was a college kid who wanted to be a biologist. I doubt he'd have that much of a hang-up over leaving a job where he was making ten dollars an hour."

"Maybe so. The point is, there's no proof. And until you find some, there's nothing else to investigate. It is what it is, an unfortunate tragedy."

8

After leaving the police station, Hall and Charlotte decided to go home and do some more computer work, hoping they could find out something else. As they walked into the apartment building, they started making plans.

"Your apartment or mine?" Charlotte asked.

Hall shrugged. "I dunno. Does it matter?"

Once they were off the elevator, they went to Charlotte's apartment, if only because her door came first. She jiggled the handle, as she'd always done before she opened the door, just to make sure it was still locked. Much to her surprise, it wasn't locked. She turned the handle, and the door opened. She looked on in shock, then turned to Hall.

"I locked it. I know I did."

"Maybe you just forgot this time," Hall said, not

really concerned yet. "Maybe you were rushing and thought you did."

"No, I know I locked it. I remember turning the knob before I left. It was definitely locked."

Now a little more alarmed, Hall put his hand on Charlotte's arm to move her off to the side so he could go in first. He pushed the door open wider and stepped into the apartment. Almost immediately he could see the damage. There were books, papers, and magazines littered all over the floor.

"Is everything OK?" Charlotte asked.

Hall didn't respond, instead moving further into the apartment, not sure if anyone was still there. He quickly checked the kitchen and cleared it, allowing himself to move on to the bedrooms. He thoroughly checked both bedrooms and the bathroom, but didn't see any signs of an intruder. They were long gone. He came back over to the front door to get Charlotte.

"All right, it's safe to come in now."

Charlotte walked in and her mouth dropped at seeing her apartment look like a tornado ripped through it. "Oh my... what did they do?"

"More importantly, why did they do it?"

"What do you mean?"

"Well, you're not on the first floor. This apartment isn't the easiest of targets. If you're gonna snatch and run, you do it on the first floor, not the third. Whoever did this was looking for something specific."

"Like what? What would they be looking for?"

"I don't know. Any unhappy clients of yours lately?"

"Really? I don't have unhappy clients. I do design and advertising stuff. If someone doesn't like something, I just fix it."

"I guess you should go through everything," Hall said. "Find out if anything's missing."

"I don't like this."

"Nobody likes being robbed."

"What if this has to do with Keith Zeller?"

"I think that's kind of a big jump to make right now. It's not like we've really rattled anyone's cage or anything."

"What if we did?" Charlotte asked. "What if we did, and we didn't know it?"

"Yeah, well, I've been right along with you the entire time and nothing's happened to me."

Charlotte raised one eyebrow. "You sure about that?"

Hall thought about it for a minute, then suddenly left the apartment, Charlotte trailing right behind him. They went down the hallway to his apartment. Once they got there, Hall already knew he was walking into a similar situation. His door wasn't even completely closed. And he knew he'd locked it. It was open just a hair. Before going in, he directed Charlotte to wait in the hall, just outside the door.

Hall then pushed the door open and walked in. He

noticed the same kind of mess on his floor. He was only able to look around for a few seconds before he was hit in the back of the head, causing him to crash down onto the floor. A masked man stood overtop of him. Hall slowly rolled over onto his back and looked up at his intruder, who looked like he was about to unleash some more punishment on him. Hall quickly regained his senses and kicked the man's feet out, making him fall to the floor as well. Hall jumped on top of the man and started drilling him with punches. The masked man was having trouble fighting back. Luckily for him he had help. Another masked man came flying in from the kitchen and tackled Hall.

As Hall and the second man wrestled around on the floor, the first man got back to his feet, ready to help out and outnumber their skillful opponent. Hall was doing a good job thwarting the two men, taking turns as to which one was receiving his powerful kicks and punches. He was obviously the better individual fighter. It was just a question of how long he could successfully hold off the two men. It turned out to be a moot point, as another masked man came out of the bedroom, hitting Hall in the back of the head with something hard, which wound up being the handle of a pistol.

Hearing all the commotion going on inside, Charlotte couldn't stand there any longer, listening to Hall get his lunch handed to him. It was obvious he needed help. Though Hall had picked himself up again and was doing an admirable job of fighting off three men, it was just too much for him. The intruders were slowly getting the upper hand. Charlotte called the police to report what was going on, but they probably wouldn't get there for a few minutes. That was enough time for them to kill Hall if that's what they had in mind. She couldn't let him take a beating without trying to help him.

Charlotte rushed inside the apartment and jumped on the back of one of the men, putting her arm around the man's throat. He took a few steps back as he wriggled around, trying to get the woman off him. Charlotte squeezed her arm around the man's throat to cinch it in deeper. The man thrashed around and threw his arms up to try to hit her, but he wasn't getting much force behind his blows. The other two men, figuring their partner could handle the woman, kept their attention on Hall, continuing their fight with him.

Eventually, the man with Charlotte on his back figured he wasn't getting her off him. Plus, he was starting to have difficulty breathing with her forearm pressed against his throat. He stumbled back, but regained his balance before falling over. He then saw the wall and turned around, going backwards as fast as he could until he rammed into the wall. Charlotte groaned at the impact of hitting the wall, though her back absorbed most of it. She still wasn't relinquishing her grip. The man leaned forward a few times and kept repeatedly hitting the wall, hoping one of the blows would eventually get Charlotte off of him. He had no such luck, however. She was not letting go.

"Help!" the man yelled, though it was barely more than a whisper with Charlotte's grip on his throat.

One of the men looked over and shook his head. "Can't even take care of one woman?"

With the third man having the upper hand on Hall at the moment, the second intruder went over to Charlotte and grabbed her by the hair, pulling her off the man's back. Charlotte quickly got to her feet and slapped the man as hard as she could. The man put his hand up to his cheek, thinking she had a pretty powerful slap. Charlotte tried hitting him a few more times, but that only served to infuriate the man more. He picked Charlotte up by the throat and carried her across the living room until they got to one of the wooden end tables and choke slammed her down on the table, breaking it under the weight of Charlotte's body.

"How you like that, bitch?" the man said, somewhat gleefully.

In as much pain as she could ever remember, Charlotte couldn't do anything except lay there. She let out a few moans and groans, but she could barely move. It felt like every bone in her body was broken. In reality, she was fine, other than the pain that came with getting thrown through a table. She took the bump like a championship pro wrestler, though she was out of commission for the rest of this fight.

Hall had gotten the upper hand again against his man, but that was only short-lived, as the other two came over to help out now that they were done with Charlotte. Hall did his best to fend the three men off, but they eventually got the better of him and got him off his feet, kicking and punching him as he lay face down on the ground. They continued with the assault for another minute or two, just to make sure that the dangerous man was completely out of the fight. Once they were done with the beat down, two of the men picked Hall up and held his arms from behind, while the leader of the group proceeded to punch Hall in the face a few more times.

"How's that feel, huh?"

Hall turned his head and spit some blood out. "Feels like my grandmother hits harder than you."

The man laughed. "Oh, a smart guy, huh?" The man punched him a few more times for being a smartass. "That do something for that smart mouth of yours?"

Hall mustered up a smile, then spit some more blood out, this time landing on the man's shirt.

"You know what we're doing here?"

"You the new interior decorators I hired?" Hall replied.

He got another shot across his jaw for that one.

"Stop what you're working on. Do something else. For your own well-being."

"I'm flattered you care so much about me."

"I don't. If it was up to me, you wouldn't be getting up from here. We wouldn't even be having this conversation. But my boss is trying to be diplomatic. They want to at least give you a chance before we kill you."

"Nice of them. Who would that boss be? I'd like to thank him."

"You can thank him by telling Zeller's sister that her brother died the way the police said he did."

"I'll have to think about it."

The man punched Hall in the stomach a few times just for fun. He was about to do it a few more times, but now police sirens were blaring in the background. That was probably the only thing stopping the man from continuing to use Hall's head as a punching bag.

"Jer, we gotta go. Cops," the man that choke slammed Charlotte said.

"Saved by the bell." It wasn't really so though, as the man unleashed a few parting shots for Hall to remember him by. "Stay off the Keith Zeller case. Or the next time you won't be as lucky as you are now."

They threw Hall on the ground as the three men escaped, running out of the apartment before the police got there. Hall's body hugged the ground, thankful that he was still breathing. His thoughts immediately turned to Charlotte, wanting to make sure she was OK. Though he was now bleeding from a few cuts on his face, he wasn't even concerned with himself. He saw Charlotte's legs on the floor where his end table used to be and crawled over to her.

"Charlotte, you OK?"

Charlotte only groaned in reply. She then was able to muster the only words she could think of. "Did we win?"

Hall laughed. "No. No, I don't think so. I'm pretty sure we got our asses kicked."

"Oh. Felt like we won."

"Really?"

Charlotte writhed around in pain, holding her back. "How do these wrestlers get thrown around like this all the time and are still able to walk?"

"Practice."

Charlotte got to her knees and held the back of her head. "I feel like I got run over by a truck."

Hall put his arms around her and hugged her. "You'll be OK."

"You don't look so hot yourself. You're bleeding all over the place."

"Hey, I'll exchange blood for our lives still being intact any day."

"I think I need a chiropractor," Charlotte said, holding her back.

Hall kissed her on the forehead, still holding her close. "We'll figure out who's responsible for this."

"Cops should be here soon, shouldn't they?"

"Yeah, I think I heard them outside. Should be up in a minute."

"So your theory about Zeller overdosing all by himself? I'd say this is proof positive about Olivia being right."

"Yeah," Hall said, holding his ribs. "I would say I'm coming around."

9

The next day, Hall and Charlotte met back in her apartment, since hers was the least messy of the two. They spent most of the previous night trying to rest and recuperate after getting the stuffing beaten out of them. It might have helped a little, but they both still felt pretty sore. They had headaches, body aches, and every other type of ache. They tried to clean up their apartments a little, but neither had much energy to do so in their current state, so there was still stuff thrown all over the floor.

After entering Charlotte's apartment, Hall sat down gingerly on the couch next to her, still holding his ribs. His face was battered and bruised, with the complementary cuts to match. He looked like a fighter who had gone twelve rounds.

"How's your ribs?" Charlotte asked.

"Just sore. I'm thankful for no broken bones. How's your back?"

"Better. I'd still rather not do that again anytime soon—or ever again, for that matter."

"Oh, you don't want to do it again today?"

"Yeah, let's not."

Charlotte rubbed the handsome, cut up face of her boyfriend. "Your beautiful face."

"It's nothing. It'll heal."

"You look like you got thrown through the windshield of a car or something."

"Thanks for the reminder."

"So what are we gonna do about this? We obviously made someone very nervous."

"Question is, who?" Hall asked.

"Well, we spoke to three people yesterday."

"Five if you count Olivia and Bradham."

"Well, yeah, but I think we can safely rule them out," Charlotte said. "Now the question is, which one of the other three?"

"I know who my money's on."

"Who?"

"Our friendly store manager, Sharon."

"Why?"

"She was the only one of the three to really object to us looking into Keith's death. I'm not buying her story about just wanting closure for everybody. She doesn't want us looking into it because she doesn't like what we'll find."

"Yeah, you're probably right. And another thing about his roommates… if they were gonna shove a needle in Keith's arm, they probably wouldn't do it inside their apartment and leave him there. They'd probably dump him somewhere, don't you think?"

"Probably. Unless they had no choice. But I get your point."

"So what's the plan for today?"

"As long as we're both able to move around, I'd say we need to look into our friend Sharon some more," Hall replied.

"I'm good. Let's just try to avoid any more fights, OK? I think my head might explode if it gets hit again."

"I hear ya."

They started moving again and briefly got up before Hall sat back down again. Charlotte thought he might have been in too much pain and stood up too quickly.

"You all right?" She put her hands on his chest. "A lot of pain?"

"Huh? Oh, no, it's not that. I mean, yeah, there's pain, but I'm not… I just thought of something."

"What?"

"Those guys who attacked us. They left a clue."

"A clue? Like what?"

Hall thought back to the moment he was thinking of. "Just before they left, when they heard the police sirens, one of them called the other Jer. He was trying to get him to hurry up."

"Jer? His name?"

Hall looked at her and nodded. "Yeah, could be."

"Jerry? Jerome? Maybe a nickname?"

"I think maybe we should take this to Bradham, see if he could run down some names for us. Maybe he can get something."

"Then what?"

"Well, if he comes up with something, then maybe we can pay this Jer a visit," Hall said. "And if not, then I think we should go visit the pharmacy again to let our friendly store manager know we're not going away."

"That could do two things. One, it could scare her away and we never see her again. Or two, it could provoke another visit from our friends from last night."

"Either way, then we'll know who's pulling the strings."

They got themselves ready and left the apartment to go down to the police station. Charlotte seemed to be in a little better state, so she did the driving. That left Hall in the passenger seat, able to observe their surroundings more closely. That led to him noticing a familiar blue sedan that was in back of them. After a few minutes, Charlotte noticed him constantly shifting around in his seat, turning around, looking in the side mirror, seeming very fidgety.

"What's the matter with you?"

Hall turned around again. "I think we're being followed."

"Oh great. It's probably those jerks from last night."

"Could be."

"What are we gonna do?"

"Nothing. Just keep driving."

"Why would they be following us?"

"Probably to see if we're still on the case or not," Hall answered.

"Well, they're gonna know that as soon as we go to the police station."

"Not necessarily. They might think we're following up on yesterday's incident."

"What if they try to do something before we get there? I'm not a stunt car driver, you know."

"Just relax and don't panic. Keep on driving like you normally would so they don't think we're on to them."

"I hate this."

Hall smiled. "How do you like investigative work now?"

"Shut up. It's still the right thing to do."

"Could be. It doesn't come without a price though."

"Yeah, well, hopefully last night is the only time we'll pay for it."

Hall nodded. That was a statement he could get behind. "Let's get through this and deliver a bill of our own."

They kept on driving to the police station, not speeding up or driving erratically. They didn't want whoever was following them to know that they were spotted yet. As long as the car kept their distance and didn't try to engage them somehow, there was no need for them to do anything different. Hall kept his eye on them the entire drive. It didn't even seem like that good of a tail, he thought. They usually were only a car or two behind them the entire way there, not exactly keeping themselves inconspicuous. Nonetheless, Charlotte drove as she usually would, not trying to shake them.

Hall was eager to see what would happen when they eventually reached the police station. Would the car behind them follow them in? Or would they just keep on going? Once they were about five minutes away, a new idea popped into Charlotte's head.

"Hey, I just thought of something. What if these guys are cops?"

"Cops?" Hall replied.

"Yeah. What if they're keeping an eye on us in case something else happened?"

"Yeah, I guess that's possible. Could always swing it by Bradham when we talk to him."

A few minutes later, they finally pulled into the police parking lot. The car behind them just kept on going though.

"Guess that solves that," Hall said.

"What?"

"If they were police, wouldn't they have followed us in?"

"Not necessarily," Charlotte answered. "Maybe they're just trying to maintain their cover."

Hall had his doubts, but maybe it could've been. Who was he to say definitively one way or the other? Once they checked in at the main desk, with Bradham's clearance, they were given their visitor passes and were allowed to roam the building in order to find the detective. Bradham was in his office like he usually was. He was standing by a file cabinet, putting some folders away as his two visitors walked in.

"Hey, what can I do for you?"

"Well, for starters, you got a couple guys following us?" Hall asked.

"What are you talking about?"

"On our way here, I noticed a car following us. Thought maybe you ordered someone to keep an eye on us after what happened yesterday."

"Oh, yeah, I heard about that," Bradham said. "Glad to see you both look none the worse for wear."

"Yeah, thanks. Anyway, is that your tail?"

"Don't know anything about it."

"You don't?"

"Nope. If you're being followed, it's not us."

"You're sure?" Hall asked, not liking the alternative.

"Listen, Brandon, when you were here a couple months ago with the train thing, I didn't have enough men then to keep an eye on you, and guess what, I still don't. Unless you're a key witness in a court case, right now, you're on your own. We're backlogged, swamped, under water, and every other adjective you can think of to describe how far behind we are."

Bradham finally found the files he was looking for and forcefully shut the file cabinet drawer. He walked over to his desk and tossed the folders down, looking a little frustrated.

"Bad day at the office?" Hall asked.

"These days... they're all bad days. Like I said, we're so far behind... I don't even have the time to sit here and talk to you, so whatever you want, you better make it fast."

"Well, it's about our incident yesterday."

"What about it?"

"I remembered something. Thought maybe it could help identify who it was."

"What do you remember?"

"The leader of the group was called Jer. I don't know if it's short for Jerry, or Jerome, or something else, but it's a start."

"That's not really much to start with," Bradham said. "You know how many people have a name that starts with that? Could also be Jeremy, Jeremiah, Jerell, Jermane, Jerod..."

"OK, I get your point."

"And that's only if they liked the guy. Maybe they were calling him a jerk. Maybe it's short for jerk. Or maybe he's from Jersey. Ever think of that?"

Hall sighed, realizing that Bradham was having some fun with it, though he was also correct. It could have been just about anything.

"Or maybe it's a last name. Could be Jericho, Jerrett, Jerowski, Jeronimo…"

"OK, Steve, I get your point."

Bradham looked at the pair, then wiped his forehead, appearing frustrated himself. "Look, I'm not trying to be a prick, but having three letters of a name isn't much to work with."

"So you won't look into it?" Charlotte asked.

"I didn't say that. I just said it isn't much to work with. Could lead in a thousand different directions. But I will look into it."

"Great. When?"

"At some point," Bradham said, pointing to the folders and papers on his desk. "Can't guarantee it'll be today, but at some point, I'll look into it."

"Well, that doesn't really help us, Steve," Hall said. "Whoever roughed us up yesterday, if they're the ones following us, and they know we're here, they know we're not off the case."

"Most likely."

"Well, that also means they're gonna come back and try again. And this time, they'll try to finish the job."

"Again, probably right."

"So we're just supposed to sit back and wait for you to clear your schedule?"

"What do you want from me?" Bradham asked.

"A little help would be nice."

"Brandon, look, you know I'm swamped. I don't

even have the time to go to the men's room without it backing me up an additional day. If you wanna look into it in the meantime, be my guest."

"How are we gonna do that?"

"I'll set you up on a computer. You can go through mug shots and files, see if you can pick the guy out."

"They were wearing masks," Hall said.

"All you're looking for is a name. See if anything matches."

"Well, that's great if he's been convicted of something. What if he's fresh out of the criminal academy?"

"In that case you're out of luck. And if that's the case, there's nothing else I'd be able to do either."

"Fine."

Bradham could see his visitors didn't like his answer, but there really wasn't much else he could do. "Hey, that's the best I can do right now. It's better than nothing."

Hall and Charlotte looked at each other. "It is better than nothing," Charlotte said.

"Yeah, I guess. I just hope this person is in there."

"What if he's not?"

"Then we go back to the drawing board."

10

Hall and Charlotte spent the next several hours looking through files of known criminals, hoping something would jump out at them. Unfortunately, nothing did.

"Can you believe how many criminals there are with the letters J-E-R?" Charlotte asked.

"Between first names and last names, more than I can count. I had a feeling this would be a wild-goose chase."

"What if we can whittle it down further?"

"How so?"

"Well, take a guess at how tall the guy was and then we can eliminate people taller or shorter than that range."

"You do realize I was either on the ground, on my knees, or fighting several guys at once to pay much attention to how tall he was, right?" Hall asked.

"Just a thought."

"And even if I took a guess, there's no guarantee that I'd even be close to accurate. We could wind up eliminating the one guy who actually was there."

"Yeah, you're right."

"It's a good thought though."

"If only they weren't wearing masks," Charlotte said.

"Yeah, that would make it a lot easier, wouldn't it?"

"What do we do now?"

Hall continued staring at the screen, not wanting to give up on it yet, even though it was looking impossible. "You know what we should do?"

"What?"

"Dig into the backgrounds of all these people and find out who has a connection to our friend Sharon."

"That's gonna take time."

"I know, but what other choice do we have?" Hall asked.

"What if none of them do?"

Hall shrugged. "Then maybe we got this thing all wrong. Maybe we find a connection to one of the roommates. I don't know. Somewhere, one of these people made a friend request with those bozos who jumped us. It's gotta be out there for us to find somewhere."

"I can start writing the names down," Charlotte said.

"Wait a minute. There's a few hundred names

there; that'll take forever. Let's find Bradham again and see if he can just print it out for us."

The pair got up and walked back into the detective's office again. Bradham was sitting at his desk and talking on the phone as the pair sat down in front of him, patiently waiting for him to finish up.

After a few minutes, Bradham hung up the phone. "You guys again? What do you want now?"

"Hey, just 'cause you're having a hard day doesn't mean you gotta take it out on us," Hall said. "We didn't do anything to cause your shortage of manpower."

"You're right, I'm sorry. What can I do for you?" the detective asked, much more pleasantly this time.

"Well, we looked through those files."

"Find anything?"

Hall shrugged. "Who can tell? Maybe he's there, I dunno."

"So?"

"So we'd like to get a printout of those names so we can dig deeper into their backgrounds, figure out if there's a connection to the pharmacy manager, or Zeller's roommates, for that matter."

"Sorry, no can do."

"What? Why not?"

"Because those are official police records, and they cannot leave the building in the hands of nonofficial personnel."

"Well, that's ridiculous, we were just looking at

them, anyway. What difference does it make?" Hall asked.

"The difference is it's against policy."

"Well, that's stupid."

"I don't make the rules, Brandon, I just follow them."

"If you want, we can sit at that computer and write them all down by hand if that makes you feel better," Charlotte said.

That statement got an evil-looking glance from Bradham.

"And it means that we'll be here for the next several hours, probably popping in here every few minutes with any questions we have. Wouldn't it make more sense to just print it out and give it to us so we can get out of here and be out of your hair?"

"What hair? Another two weeks of this and I won't have any."

"That's my point. If you just print it out for us, we can be on our way and you can go back to what you were doing. Unless you wanna dig into the background of all these names for us?"

Bradham rolled his eyes and sighed, feeling like he was being railroaded. "You really feel like there's a connection here somewhere?"

"I don't know. Doesn't hurt to look, does it? I mean, if you hire thugs to scare people and beat them up, you usually don't just find them in the phone book, do you? You usually have to know them from somewhere."

Bradham rubbed his face and sighed again. Right now, he would have agreed to just about anything to get them out of his office so he could get back to what he was doing. Hall and Charlotte then both spoke up at the same time and kept on talking, hoping to convince the detective to see it their way.

"All right," Bradham said, instantly silencing his guests. "Fine. I'll print the damn thing out for you."

That drew a smile from both Hall and Charlotte. "Thank you," Hall said.

"But I never gave it to you."

"Just happened to find it outside on the pavement somewhere."

"And when you're done with it, you need to get rid of it."

"I'll put it right in the fireplace and watch it burn."

"Do you even have a fireplace?" Bradham asked.

"Well, no, but... I'll put it in the shredder, OK? I got one of those. Rip it up into a thousand little pieces and nobody will ever see it again after that. OK?"

"Yeah, sure."

Bradham started typing on his computer, bringing up the same information the pair was just looking at a few minutes earlier. Once he had it, he printed the sheets and handed it over.

"You really think you're gonna find a connection in there?"

"Don't know," Hall replied. "Sure gonna try though. We've only spoken to four people about this. Zeller's sister, his two roommates, and his manager. Now all of a sudden, a few goons show up at our apartments, wreck both our places, beat us into oblivion, nearly kill us, and I'm supposed to think that's some sort of coincidence?" Hall shook his head. "Sorry, not buying it. One of them knows more than they're letting on."

"And you're thinking it's the manager?"

"Well, she was the most obstinate, the least friendly, the only one who seemed to accept he overdosed himself, and the one who seemed the least happy to see us. So yeah, she's at the top of my list."

"It's a big jump to make, Brandon. Going from a small store manager with no police record, to carrying out a murder and having a goon squad on the payroll to rough you up."

"I know. But it's all I got right now. One of these people talked to somebody. If they're not directly involved, they must know someone who is."

"Better be careful. If there's someone following you like you say, they're not gonna like you being here."

"Believe me, I know."

"Now if there's nothing else I can do for you guys, I really do need to get back to work."

"Thanks, Steve, we owe you."

"Yeah, yeah, get out of here." Hall and Charlotte rose and then walked over to the door. Bradham stopped them just before they left. "Hey."

"Yeah?"

"If you find anything, let me know."

Hall smiled and nodded. They walked out of the police station and went back to their car. They looked around to see if they could see the same blue car hanging around, though there was no sign of it.

"Where to?" Charlotte asked. "Back to the apartment?"

"You know what? Let's go back and visit our friendly pharmacy and talk to Sharon again."

"What for?"

"I wanna see if I can rattle her cage a little."

"You think it'll do any good?"

"Who knows? Can't hurt."

They pulled out of the police parking lot, and within a few minutes of being on the road, Hall casually glanced in the side mirror and noticed that familiar blue car a few car lengths behind them, separated by one vehicle in between. Charlotte heard him sigh and wondered what the problem was.

"What's wrong?"

"Looks like we got company again," Hall answered.

Charlotte looked in the rearview mirror. "I see them. What do you wanna do?"

"Just keep driving. We'll see how they wanna play it."

"What if they try to make a move on us?"

"Then we'll handle it."

"You really think we're gonna get any different answers out of Sharon than we got before?"

"Who knows?" Hall replied. "When pressed with

crucial information and evidence that we know what she's saying is a lie, some people crack under the pressure."

"She doesn't seem like the flappable type to me."

"Maybe. If she had Keith killed though, that sounds like she got nervous over something and cracked, doesn't it?"

"Yeah, I guess."

"Let's see if we can do the same."

11

The blue car followed them all the way to the pharmacy. When Hall and Charlotte pulled into the rear parking lot of the building, they got out and stood by their car for a moment, waiting for the other car to drive by, hoping to get a look at the occupants. The blue car did drive by, but they weren't able to make out who was inside. All they could tell was that it looked like two men: one in the driver's seat, and the other in the passenger side.

"I'm sure we'll be seeing them again," Charlotte said.

"No question about that."

The two of them went inside, immediately greeted by the same cashier as the last time they visited. Instead of walking around this time, they asked to speak to Sharon right away. Sharon appeared within a minute, and they could see her coming down the aisle. As soon as she saw the pair, her shoulders slumped, instantly looking dejected at having to talk to them again.

"You don't look happy to see us," Hall said. "Or maybe you're just surprised."

"I am surprised," Sharon replied. "I thought I told you everything yesterday."

"Not quite. You can tell us who those goons are that you sent after us."

"Excuse me?"

"After we left here, we went back home to our apartments only to find they'd been broken into and our things trashed. Not only that, we found three men inside who nearly killed the both of us."

A look of surprise came over Sharon's face. Hall couldn't quite tell if it was genuine, or she was just plastering it on. "I'm sorry to hear that."

"Yeah, well, I don't want sorry's. I want answers."

"And you think I can tell you anything?"

"Yeah, I do."

"If you're thinking I sent them, I can assure you that I didn't. Why would I do that?"

"Because from the moment we met yesterday, you were adamant about Keith's death not being suspicious."

"Because that's how I feel. Not because I have something to hide."

"So it's just a coincidence that after we talked to you someone jumped us?"

"It must be. I wouldn't have any reason to do that."

"Maybe you got something to hide," Charlotte said. "Maybe there really is something funny with Keith's death and you know it."

"And maybe you just have a lot of guesses and no proof."

"We'll get it."

"Well, you won't get any that involves me," Sharon replied. "Because I haven't done anything. I liked Keith. I was his boss. He was a good worker. But that's the extent of our relationship. What reason would I even have to do that?"

"Maybe you two had an inappropriate relationship," Hall said.

"I'm married."

"In this day and age, you think that really matters? All the more reason to get rid of him if you did."

"You know, I'm not going to stand here and subject myself to your slanderous accusations. You have no proof. And until you get some, don't ever talk to me again. Unless it's through my attorney. Is that clear?"

"Perfectly."

Sharon walked away as Hall, and Charlotte stood near the counter, watching her leave. Hall sighed, not pleased with how the conversation went. He was hoping to get a few more answers out of her.

"We went in too hot and heavy," Hall said. "Should've massaged her a little more."

"You really think that would've made a difference?"

"I don't know. Maybe not. I didn't even get to ask her if she knew anyone with the letters J-E-R."

"She's right, you know," Charlotte said. "We don't have any proof."

"We'll have to get some, won't we?"

"We might be wasting a lot of time if she really didn't do it."

"Well, we gotta start somewhere, don't we? And I'd say she's as good an option as any."

"Yeah."

"Let's get out of here."

Hall and Charlotte walked out of the pharmacy. As soon as they exited the building, they noticed men on both sides of the door, just standing against the wall. Hall quickly glanced at them, not liking the look of them. He then looked at the cars in the parking lot and noticed the blue sedan that had been following them. Knowing these guys were likely to do something while Hall and Charlotte's backs were turned, Hall wanted to get the jump on them. He turned to the one on his right and started fumbling through his pocket.

"Hey, buddy, you got a light?" Hall asked.

"No, sorry."

"That's all right."

Hall took his hand out of his pocket and uncorked a powerful right hand that connected to the side of the man's temple. The shock of the blow sent the man to the ground. Charlotte let out a scream, then took a few steps back as the other man charged past her, trying to get to Hall. Hall turned around and saw him coming, delivering a backward thrust kick to the man's stomach, taking the wind out of him.

Assuming these two men were part of the group that attacked him in his apartment, this fight would go down differently. Hall was ready for this one. He was able to get in the first blow. Hall turned his attention back to the first man, who'd gotten back to his feet. Hall ducked and blocked a few punches, then used his martial arts training to decimate the man, hitting him with more punches and kicks than he could count. The man was down and out within a minute. The second man got his wind back and charged at Hall again, even getting a punch or two in. But it wasn't long before Hall had gotten the upper hand. Just like the first man, Hall used his martial arts abilities to dismantle the man, making quick work of him. With his job complete, Hall took a step back and looked down at the carnage.

"Do you need help with anything?" Charlotte joked.

Hall smiled. "I think I got it all under control."

Charlotte interlocked her fingers together and cracked her knuckles. "Oh, that's a shame. I was just getting warmed up."

"I'm sure you were."

"You hogged them all for yourself. That's very selfish of you. You didn't leave any for me."

"Don't worry, next time I'll step back and let you do it all."

"Well, I mean, I don't want to take away all your fun or anything." They both looked at each other and smiled. "I called the cops while you were busy. Should be here in a minute."

"Good," Hall replied.

While they were waiting, Hall went over to the two men, still down on the ground, and went through their pockets, wanting to make sure they weren't armed and could hurt them before the police arrived. He removed their wallets, and he also found a gun on each of them. Putting their guns in his belt, Hall walked over to Charlotte, rifling through their wallets to find out who they were. He was hoping one of their names had the initials he was looking for. Unfortunately, neither of them did.

"They're not the ones," Hall said.

"They might still be the other two guys that were there. Just not the head guy. If J.E.R. is the head guy, these two might be his minions. The top guy always sends the B Squad in to take care of things."

"Yeah, maybe."

The police came a few minutes later, and after they were informed of the situation, they took the two men into custody. By then, a small crowd had formed, including the people in the pharmacy. Sharon was standing just outside the door looking at the festivities. As the crowd started to disperse, and the police had the men inside their patrol car, Hall and Sharon locked eyes.

"You don't happen to know them, do you?" Hall asked.

A disgusted look came over Sharon's face as she retreated back into the building.

"I think that was a no," Charlotte said.

"But was it an honest no?"

"What do you wanna do now?"

Hall didn't answer as the police car pulled out of the parking lot. He and Charlotte watched them go until they were out of sight.

"I'd say we go home and start doing a lot of legwork," Hall said.

"Checking all those names?"

Hall nodded. "Checking all those names."

"It's a good thing my ex taught me some of his hacking skills. I have a feeling we're gonna need them."

Hall grinned. "I agree." He looked at the pharmacy building, getting a thought in his head. "You know, maybe it'd be a good idea to check their employment records to see if they've employed, either now or in the past, someone with the initials we're looking for."

"The guy who attacked us doesn't seem like the kind who would work in a place like this."

"Maybe not. Worth a shot though."

"I have a feeling this is gonna be a long night," Charlotte said.

"I agree. Before we go home, we need to stop for a pizza."

"Pizza? Why?"

"Because you're right, it's gonna be a long night."

12

Hall and Charlotte spent the rest of the night in her apartment, on their computers, trying to find a connection somewhere. They didn't drift off to sleep until around two in the morning. At that point, they still hadn't found the clue they were looking for. Hall woke up the next morning around ten, picking his head up off the kitchen table where he fell asleep. The aroma of the coffee must have done the trick. He groggily opened his eyes and saw Charlotte standing in the kitchen. Once she saw his eyes open, she came over and gave him a kiss, along with putting a cup of coffee down in front of him.

"Thanks," Hall said, taking a sip, hoping it would help to wake him up. "How long you been up?"

"About an hour."

Hall yawned and stretched his arms out. "Man, I'm tired."

"Well, we did have a late night."

Hall looked down at the papers in front of him and started shuffling them around, not remembering where he left off. He kept yawning, making him think he should finish his coffee before getting back to work. He looked up at Charlotte, who had a smug look on her face. It was the kind of look someone had when they were holding in a secret, happy to torment someone with the knowledge that they knew something that nobody else did.

"What?" Hall asked, looking down at his clothes. "Did I drool on my shirt or something?"

Charlotte laughed. "No. I found something."

"You did? With the case?"

Charlotte nodded. "I actually found it about half an hour ago. I just started looking through things after I put the coffee on and was waiting for you to wake up."

"What is it?"

Charlotte grabbed the paper off the counter and placed it next to Hall's cup of coffee, then sat down next to him. "There it is."

Hall looked at it, though he wasn't sure what he was supposed to be seeing. "What am I looking at?"

"His name is Jerry Guzman."

"OK? How'd you lock in on this guy?"

"Look at the notes I wrote down at the bottom. He's twenty-nine years old, has a record, he was in prison for three years from the age of twenty-two to twenty-five, aaaand... the real kicker? He's been employed at the pizza shop that Brian works at for over a year."

"And you think this is the guy we're looking for?" Hall asked.

"Look at his description. Same type of build, right? Has a connection to one of the people we talked to. Everything fits, doesn't it?"

Hall nodded as he read the paper, periodically taking sips of his coffee. "Yeah. Sure looks like it."

"I think we need to take a trip down to that pizza place and talk to him."

"I agree. But not now."

"Why not?"

"Because I don't think they open until twelve."

"Oh. Well, after that." Hall looked at his girlfriend and smiled. "What?"

"You're beautiful. You know that?"

Charlotte smiled, then threw her arms around him. "It's always nice to hear." They then started kissing.

"This is always a better wake-up call."

"What, you don't like the taste of my coffee?"

"Not as much as I like the taste of some other things."

They continued kissing for a few more minutes, eventually pulling themselves away from each other before things escalated down a path they had not yet traveled.

"Thank you," Charlotte said.

"For what?"

"For not pushing me or rushing me into something I'm not ready for yet. I know a lot of guys, and some girls too, just wanna jump into each other's pants the moment they meet someone. I've never been that way."

Hall smiled. "It's fine. I'm not in a hurry."

"I just wanna make sure we're ready for that and it's special, you know?"

Hall put his hand on her chin and gently kissed her lips. "I'll wait as long as you want. It'll be worth it."

"You're a different kind of guy, you know that?"

"Maybe because you're a different kind of girl."

"Different in a weird way?"

"Different in a special way. You like to help people. Even if it puts you in danger as a result. That's a special quality that not everyone has."

"Well, she's a friend..."

"I'm not even talking about this case specifically," Hall said. "Even if we go back to when you met me. I can't imagine a lot of people would've done what you did."

Charlotte shrugged. "I just did what I thought was right."

Hall smiled, then gave her another kiss. "And that's what makes you special."

They waited a couple hours before going back to the pizza place. When they got there, they saw the same man at the counter as the last time they were there, the owner of the place. They walked up to him as he was writing something down on a pad of paper. He looked up, instantly recognizing them.

"Hey, I remember you guys. You're the ones looking into Keith's death, right?"

"That's right," Hall replied.

"How you making out on that?"

"It's coming along."

"Good to hear it. What can I get ya?"

"Some information."

"Hey, I don't talk to anybody who's not a paying customer. I'm running a business here. You want information it's gonna cost you," he said with a laugh.

"How much?"

"Whatever you wanna order."

Hall smiled and looked at Charlotte. "All right, we'll get a couple slices."

"My man. Take a seat at one of the tables, and I'll bring it right over to you and then we can talk."

Hall and Charlotte found a nearby table in the nearly empty establishment. Since it hadn't been open long, there were only two other tables that had people sitting at them. Most of their business came from dinner up until they closed at midnight.

"They actually have pretty good pizza," Charlotte said.

"Yeah, not too bad."

A few minutes later, the owner came over with a tray. He sat down and handed each of them a plate, along with one for himself. He also gave them each a soda.

"We didn't ask for this," Hall said, holding the soda up.

"I know. My compliments. You can't have a pizza without something to wash it down, you know?"

The three of them sat there, eating their food, talking about pizza. Actually, talking about anything else other than what they were there for. After they were done eating, Hall took a sip of his drink before getting down to their real business.

"So we wanted to talk to you about an employee of yours, Jerry Guzman."

The owner's face sank immediately upon hearing the name. It didn't seem like it brought up good memories. It didn't go unnoticed.

"You know him, right?"

"Sure, I know him. I mean, he hasn't been gone that long."

"What do you mean, that long?" Hall asked. "He's not still working here?"

"No, afraid not. He last worked here a few months ago. Maybe three months, something like that."

"Why'd he leave? You know?"

"I fired him. Shame. Gave him a chance. Just couldn't seem to make it work."

"What kind of chance?" Charlotte asked.

"Well, he was a young kid, had a police record,

figured I'd give him a chance to get back on his feet. You know how it is."

"Just didn't take advantage, huh?" Hall said.

"Well, that's the thing. He did all right for a while. Maybe a year or so he was doing pretty good. Always on time, never called out, seemed like he was really trying to make something of it."

"I take it something changed?"

"Yeah, about three months ago. Started showing up late, calling out, then the real big thing. He started showing up smelling like alcohol, drugs. Can't have that. Tried to straighten him out, give him some time to kick it, but just seemed like he couldn't do it. Eventually I had no choice. Had to let him go."

"What kind of drugs?" Charlotte asked.

"Just marijuana. At least that's all I could tell. Maybe there was other things, I don't know. But I tell everyone who works for me, I don't care what you do outside of here as far as drinking and drugs, but you don't bring it in here. We work with food all day, huh? I can't have workers showing up smelling like drugs, having it spread to the pizza, you know? I can't be serving my customers a pot pizza."

The three of them had a good laugh. "I'm sure it's been done before," Hall said.

"Maybe so. But not in a respectable joint." The three looked at each other and laughed again. "Pot, joint, I'm making jokes and I don't even know it. Maybe I should go on the road with a comedy act, huh?"

"Maybe so."

"What else can you tell us about him? He was friends with Brian?"

"Yeah, I mean, they weren't real close or anything as far as I know. They were friendly with each other when they were here, but I'm not sure if they ever hung out together outside of here."

"What about Keith?" Charlotte asked. "Did he and Guzman know each other?"

"Oh, yeah. Like I said before, Keith was a regular here. And since he and Brian were roommates, Jerry would sometimes go over and talk with them, sure."

"They get along?"

"As far as I know. I never heard any of them raising their voices or anything."

"Do you have Guzman's address?" Hall asked.

"Yeah, sure, I got it in one of my files. Why? You think Jerry got something to do with Keith's death?"

"We're not really sure at this point. We're just trying to blanket everyone who came into contact with him and see what shakes down from the tree."

"I see. Well, I can get it for you if you want."

"I'd appreciate it."

The owner left, only to return about three minutes later with a piece of paper in his hand. Written down was Guzman's address.

"Thank you," Hall said, taking the paper from him.

"I don't think Jerry's a bad kid," the owner said. "I'd be surprised if he was mixed up in this."

"Did you ever notice Jerry having discussions with anyone else?" Charlotte asked. "Maybe someone who looked like bad news? Either inside or outside?"

The owner thought for a minute. "No, not that I can recall."

"Well, thanks," Hall said. They were about to get up and leave when the owner stopped them.

"Wait a minute. I do remember one thing. It was… maybe two or three weeks, maybe a month before I let him go. He was on his break, so he went outside for a few minutes. I happened to go out a few minutes after that, just to get some fresh air. I saw him talking to some other guy near the corner of the building. Looked like they were getting into it pretty good."

"It was heated?"

"Seemed like it. They were both waving their arms around like they were both trying to make a point or something."

"You didn't happen to hear what they were talking about, did you?"

"Nah. Hey, that's one thing I don't ever do: put my nose in other people's business."

"Well, thanks a lot."

"No problem. Anytime you wanna talk more business, you let me know, huh?"

"Will do."

Hall and Charlotte finished their drinks as they watched the owner go back to his business.

"You think he has anything else to say?" Charlotte asked.

Hall laughed. "No. I think he just wants to sell us more pizza. Like he says, he's a businessman."

"Should we go pay a visit to Mr. Guzman?"

Hall nodded. "Yeah. I think that's the next step."

13

Guzman's apartment was about a fifteen-minute drive from the pizza shop. Judging by the surroundings, it wasn't one of the top complexes in the area. It looked a little run-down, graffiti on the walls, and some sketchy looking people standing out front.

"Imagine what this place looks like at night," Charlotte said.

"Doesn't give you warm and fuzzy feelings, huh?"

"Not at all. I think this place would give a nightmare a good name."

Hall laughed. "You wanna wait here for me?"

"Are you kidding? You want me to stay here by myself?"

"What could happen?"

Charlotte looked at him like he was crazy. "Seriously? What *couldn't* happen?"

"So you're not staying here?"

"How many times do I have to tell you that in some strange way, the safest place to be is always right behind you?"

"And back at the apartment?" Hall asked, remembering they had it pretty rough not too long ago.

"We made it out, right?"

"That's not really a strong lead-in."

"Oh well."

Charlotte got out of the car, still holding the paper with Guzman's address in her hand. She moved around to the front of the car to wait for Hall, and she could feel that the eyes of the scuzzy men in front of the building were watching her. She glanced over at them and confirmed that they were indeed looking at her. She turned and looked at Hall.

"Can you please hurry up so we can get this over with?"

"Why, what's the matter?" Hall asked, a hint of a laugh in his question.

"I can already feel like these people out front wanna come over and rob me or something."

Hall shook his head. "They're probably just mesmerized by your beauty. They probably haven't seen anyone as pretty as you around here lately."

Charlotte rolled her eyes. "Laying it on a little thick there, aren't you, buddy? It's not Valentine's Day or anything."

They both had a chuckle as they went inside the

apartment complex, going in the side door to avoid the rough-looking people in front of the building.

"What's his apartment number again?" Hall asked, leaning over to look at the paper in Charlotte's hand.

"306."

"Stairs or elevator?"

"I don't know. Which is less likely to get us shot at?"

"I know this is a rough-looking building, but we're not in a prison or something. I think we're OK with not getting shot at."

"You know, if we wind up getting shot at I'm not gonna let you live it down, right?"

"Of that I'm certain."

"Let's use the elevator," Charlotte said.

"Why?"

"Because we're less likely to run into people there than the stairs."

"Really? Why?"

"You can only fit a certain number of people in an elevator, right?"

"In theory."

"Well, you could theoretically run into a hundred people on the stairs, right?"

"I suppose so."

"And people have a tendency to hang out in stairways, sitting on steps, smoking, drinking, doing drugs."

"They do? What apartment buildings have you lived in that did all that?"

"Well, none. But that doesn't mean they don't here."

"I think you've watched too many detective noir books and movies," Hall said. "Your mind's running away with you."

"If my mind was running away from this place, I'd be right behind it."

They took the elevator, and lucky enough for Charlotte, nobody else was in it or joined them on the way to the third floor. Once the doors opened to their floor, the couple stepped off into the hallway. They looked at a door directly across from them, then looked around to see which direction they should be heading. They turned to their right and passed a few doors until they got to the one they were looking for.

"Guess this is it," Hall said. "I'd stand back if I were you."

"Why?"

"If this is one of the guys who jumped us at my apartment, he's likely not gonna react too well to us showing up here at his place. He might come out swinging."

"Or shooting."

Hall begrudgingly acknowledged the possibility. "Or shooting."

Hall was about to knock, but when he put his hand up to the door, he noticed that it wasn't completely shut. Hall then looked at Charlotte and told her to step back further. He pointed at the door and mouthed the words "open" to her. Charlotte put her thumb up and pointed her head back toward where they came from, thinking maybe they should get out of there for the moment. Hall shook his head though. They were already there. There was no time like the present to find out what was going on. He wasn't coming back later.

Hall pushed the door open, not completely sure if Guzman was in the apartment or not. There was no way the man could have known they were coming, so Hall was relatively sure it wasn't some kind of setup. Charlotte gave him a strange face, indicating she wasn't in favor of proceeding. She wanted to get out of there. She had a gut feeling that they were going to walk into something they wished they hadn't.

"Brandon," she whispered. "Let's go."

Hall shook his head. He pointed for her to go if she wanted. But that wasn't happening. That was against her personal motto of always being behind him. Hall put his head through the crack in the door that he'd just opened, not seeing anyone in sight yet. He noticed a mess on the floor. It seemed to be a theme in apartment buildings he'd been in recently. He looked at Charlotte and nodded for her to follow him inside as he pushed the door open all the way.

As Hall spun his head back around to enter the apartment, he turned just in time to get a fist hitting him in the forehead. He stumbled back against the door before regaining his balance again. He then charged at the man, spearing him in the stomach as they both crashed to the floor.

Charlotte looked on from the doorway and slapped her thighs with her hands as she looked at the pair wrestling around. "I knew this was a bad idea."

Hall and his opponent had gotten back to their feet and were trading haymakers with each other, neither man getting the upper hand. Whoever it was, it wasn't Guzman. The man Hall was fighting didn't have any type of mask to conceal his face, and was considerably older, probably in his mid-forties. After a minute, another man came racing in from the bedroom, jumping on top of Hall to separate him from the man he was fighting. As the two men started attacking Hall, Charlotte watched and sighed, knowing she was going to have to inject herself in the battle again.

"Here we go again."

There would have been a lot of people, men and women, who probably would have left to avoid a conflict, but Charlotte couldn't do that. Not to Hall. She felt responsible for any trouble he got into considering she was the one who pushed the case onto him. She couldn't run away from it. Even if it meant getting battered and bruised; they were lumps she would just have to take.

Even though Hall was doing an admirable job of defending himself against the two men and was getting in some shots of his own, Charlotte still launched herself into the fray. With the backs of the men to her, she jumped on one of them, trying to nudge her forearm under the man's chin. With only one man to deal with at the moment, it was enough to give Hall the upper hand, and he started taking over the fight with his adversary.

Though the one man struggled initially with Charlotte on his back, he eventually was able to loosen her grip around his throat and throw her off. She flipped over the man's shoulder, landing hard on the small of her back. She braced herself for whatever was about to happen next, though she was pleasantly surprised that nothing did. The man went over to Hall and pushed him over so he could help his partner get to his feet.

"C'mon, let's get out of here!" one of them said.

As Hall and Charlotte lay in their respective spots, they watched as the two men ran out of the apartment. Hall looked at his girlfriend and smiled.

"That was fun, huh?"

Charlotte didn't look amused. "I told you we shouldn't have come in."

They each remained where they were for a few seconds to catch their breath. Then they both got back to their feet at the same time and brushed themselves off.

"What now?" Charlotte asked.

"Well, we're already here. Might as well look around."

"Isn't this breaking and entering?"

"We didn't break anything. The door was already open."

"Oh. What if there's more of them?"

"If there were more of them, I'm sure we would've run into them already."

"You know, I was thinking, maybe you should start bringing a gun with you. Just in case."

"Maybe you should start bringing a frying pan with you. Just in case."

"Not funny. Who do you think those guys were, anyway? They weren't Guzman."

"No, they weren't."

They started looking around the apartment, checking the different rooms. Hall went into the bedroom as Charlotte checked the bathroom.

"Maybe he isn't even here," Charlotte said.

"Oh, I'm pretty sure he's here."

"How do you know?"

"Because I'm looking at him."

Charlotte left the bathroom and came rushing into the bedroom, almost running into her boyfriend as he stood there motionless. She then saw what he was looking at. Jerry Guzman. Dead. He was lying on the floor on the other side of his bed, close to the window.

"Um..." Charlotte stuttered, not sure what else to say.

"Yep."

"What are we gonna do?"

"Call the police."

"They're not gonna think we did this, are they?"

Hall looked at her and rolled his eyes. "Stop. That's like a bad movie."

"I'm just making sure."

"Call the police."

"Are you sure it wouldn't be better to just, like, get out of here and pretend we were never here?"

"Charlotte, your mind's running away with you."

"You're sure they're not gonna blame this on us? I mean, he was the guy who beat us up."

"First off, we didn't get beaten up."

"Well, it wasn't a tickle party."

"We were outnumbered," Hall said. "And we can't even be sure this was the guy who jumped us. Might have been. Might not have been too."

"So you still want me to call?"

"Yes. Hey, if we wind up going to jail, at least we're going there together, right?"

"That's not funny."

"Figured we could use the levity. Just make the call."

"Fine, I'll make the call. But if you end up going to jail, just remember I warned you."

14

After the police descended on the scene, Hall and Charlotte were instructed to wait until the detectives had talked to them. They did, waiting in the hallway as the crime scene technicians dusted for prints and did their thing. As they waited, with an officer standing guard at the door, Detective Bradham came walking down the hall. Charlotte noticed him coming and gave Hall a nudge in the arm. Hall looked up just as Bradham approached them.

"Oh, no," Bradham said. "What are you guys doing here?"

"Well..."

"As if I'm not snowed in enough right now, you gotta hand me another dead body?"

"We're just going where the investigation takes us," Hall answered.

"And it took you here?"

"Yep. Victim's name is Jerry Guzman. You remember those mug shots that you didn't give us?"

"Shhh," Bradham said, looking around. "What about them?"

"Well, he was in it."

The connection finally hit the detective. "J-E-R."

"So we had his address and came over here."

"And you killed him?"

Charlotte slapped Hall in the arm. "See? I told you!"

"I don't carry a gun, you know that," Hall said.

"Well, I just have your word for it," Bradham said. "I mean, I've never personally searched you myself."

"You can search me now if you want."

"You would've had plenty of time to ditch a weapon."

"You really think we would've hung around here if we killed him? Nobody would've known we were here."

"I think we shouldn't say another word until we've gotten a lawyer," Charlotte said.

"We don't need a lawyer," Hall replied. "He doesn't really think we're involved."

"Oh, you're involved all right," Bradham said. "Do I think you killed him? No. But you're involved. Right up to your eyeballs."

"If you don't think we killed him, then why are you grilling us like that?" Charlotte asked.

"That wasn't even close to grilling you. You have no

idea what it's like under the bright lights of an interrogation. That was child's play. Besides, I have to cross the i's and dot the t's and all that stuff and rule you out before I move on."

"Oh. OK."

"So what brought you guys here, anyway?"

"We dug into Guzman's background and found out he worked at the pizza shop that Keith went to, and the same one that his roommate works at. So we went there and found out that Guzman was fired a few months ago. The owner gave us his address, so we came here."

"Then what, you just found him lying here?"

"Umm, not quite," Hall said. "I was about to knock, saw the door was open a hair, then pushed it open. Took a few steps and was met with a right hand from somewhere."

"So just one guy?"

"No, after I started wrestling with the one guy, another guy came from somewhere. Not sure where."

"So then with your Bruce Lee moves you took both guys out?"

Hall faked a smile. "Not quite. It was a back-and-forth struggle and eventually they just split."

"Any idea who they were?"

Hall rubbed the back of his neck. "No. They were in their thirties, maybe forties. One guy had a mustache, black hair, the other guy was... just a guy. Brown hair, nothing special about him."

"Build?"

"Both probably around six feet, average build."

"Armed?" Bradham asked.

"Not that I noticed, but I guess one of them had to be if they killed Guzman."

"Well, we don't know that yet. Maybe they were here the same as you were and stumbled on him too."

"Yeah, I guess that could be possible."

"Anything else?"

"No, I think that's it."

"All right, you guys can go. If I need anything else, I'll call you."

They were about to go their separate ways when Charlotte tapped Bradham's arm. "Wait a second..."

"Think of something?" the detective asked.

"The one guy... he looked familiar."

"Which one?"

"The one with the mustache. I didn't get a great look at him, just kind of a glance, but he looked familiar, like I saw him somewhere before."

"You remember where?"

Charlotte started picking at her lip as she tried to remember. "I feel like it was recently."

"Well, that could be just about anything."

"No, it'll come to me. I have a very good memory."

"Except for faces?" Bradham said with a smile.

"Stop. Don't be funny."

"I tell you what, why don't you go home, think

about it for a while, and when it comes to you, you call me back?"

"I got it!"

Bradham looked at Hall. "That was quick."

"Good memory she says," Hall replied.

"So? What's his name?"

"I don't remember," Charlotte answered.

Bradham rolled his eyes and threw his arms up. "You just said you remembered him."

"No, I remember where I saw him. I don't remember his name."

"Well, where'd you see him?"

Charlotte looked around and then started whispering. "In the files you gave us. He was in there."

"All right, go home, look through everything again, then when you find him, you let me know."

"We will," Hall said.

Before leaving, Bradham put his hand on Hall's arm. "And just for the record, you don't need a gun to kill somebody. I've seen your handiwork up close after you were done. Those hands and feet could qualify."

"I know."

Bradham nodded. "Do me a favor?"

"What?"

"Go home and stay out of trouble, will you? You're gonna wind up backing me up until Christmas."

Hall and Charlotte smiled. "We'll do our best," Hall said. "Can't make any promises though."

"Yeah, that's what I'm afraid of."

Hall and Charlotte went back home to their apartments, though they basically just settled into hers like they usually did. They sat at her kitchen table and went through the files of mug shots that they still had, Charlotte knew exactly what she was looking for. It only took her a few minutes to find the one she wanted.

"This is it," she said.

"Found him?"

Charlotte slid the paper over halfway between them so they could both look at it together.

"Robbie Jernigan," Hall said, reading the paper. "Rough-looking guy."

"Yeah, it's him though."

"Yeah, now that I'm looking at his picture up close, this is definitely the guy."

They continued reading about Jernigan, who was a veteran of the prison system, serving ten years over a couple of different stretches. He was known to be a violent guy, having no problem using his muscle in any situation that called for it.

"Guess we should call Bradham," Charlotte said.

"Yeah."

Hall called Bradham, who wasn't that thrilled to hear from them no matter what the circumstances. He was still at the Guzman crime scene. As far as the detective was concerned, they were just making his days longer.

"What can I do for you now?" Bradham asked.

"You having a bad day?"

"I'm having a long day. They're all long. You know why? Because I keep getting pulled in different directions. Pretty soon I'll be working through my vacation at this rate."

"Sorry to hear it."

"What do you want?"

"We looked through those files and identified one of the men," Hall said.

"Oh, yeah? Who is it?"

"Guy's name is Robbie Jernigan."

"Rob Jernigan, huh?"

"You know him?"

"Yeah, I sure do. He's a known enforcer."

"For who?"

"He's a freelancer," Bradham answered. "He'll work for anybody who pays him."

"So he's not tied to any one person or anything?"

"Nope. If you got the money, he'll do a job. Any job. He's mean, has a quick temper, and doesn't mind getting down and dirty if he has to."

"You sound like you know him well."

"I've run into him a few times."

"Question is how does he fit into Keith Zeller's murder?" Hall asked.

"He doesn't."

"C'mon, Steve, you gotta admit it's looking like something's going on here."

"Come on nothing. There's zero proof right now tying any of these guys to anything. There's still no proof that Zeller was murdered. There's no proof that ties Guzman to Zeller. And there's no proof that ties Jernigan to Zeller."

"What about one of them jumping me after I started asking questions?"

"We don't even know which one it was, if either of them. Just because they got the initials, that doesn't tie them to you. Right now, all you got is a lot of theories and guesswork."

"But..."

"Listen, right now you don't have anything," Bradham said. "Doesn't mean you're wrong, doesn't mean you're not on the right path, but you're not there yet. You need some piece of evidence that ties any of these people to Zeller. Right now it's not there. We're in the evidence business. Not the throw-guesses-at-the-wall-and-see-if-it-sticks business."

Hall sighed, wanted to debate the point further, but knowing it was useless. As much as he didn't want to admit it, the detective was right. They didn't have any proof yet.

"Is this address on Jernigan good?"

"What do you mean is it good?" Bradham asked, his voice rising slightly. "They all should be good. That doesn't mean he's there though."

"Why not?"

"Listen, he just got into it with you at a crime scene,

a murder. If he thinks he can be identified, wherever he's living, he won't be there for long."

"Yeah, you're right."

"What are you thinking about, anyway? You're not thinking about paying him a visit, are you?"

"Who's not thinking about it?" Hall innocently asked.

"Brandon, don't do that. I know what's going on in your mind right now. Going to visit him is not a good idea."

"I gotta get to the bottom of this. Maybe someone paid Guzman to take out Zeller, they got wind of me and tried to do the same, then when that failed, they hired Jernigan to take out Guzman?"

"I guess in some way it's plausible. The problem is, still, there's no proof."

"Don't you think it's a little too coincidental that Zeller dies, and he's known to frequent a place Guzman works at, then he dies?"

"How many times do I gotta tell you guesswork is not proof?" Bradham asked.

"So you're not buying any of it?"

"Am I buying it? Officially, there's still nothing there. Off the record, I think you might be onto something."

"See? So going to see Jernigan is the next step. He might be able to tell us something."

"Listen to what I'm saying. That guy isn't going to

tell you anything. The only thing he's going to do is put a bullet in your head."

"You said yourself that you're backed up and you can't afford having more things on your plate."

"That doesn't mean I need help."

"I'm willing to go over and check things out for you."

"That's not what I'm saying."

Hall pretended not to hear a word the detective was saying. His mind was made up, and he wasn't going to be convinced otherwise. "All right, thanks for the approval."

"I didn't approve anything!"

"I'll let you know what I find."

"Brandon!"

"See you later."

"Brandon!"

Bradham continued shouting Hall's name a few times, but there was no one on the other end of the line. After realizing that Hall had already hung up, Bradham angrily pulled the phone away from his ear and gripped it tightly, squeezing it. He wanted to just throw it against the wall, but luckily came to his senses before he did something that stupid.

"You all right, Steve?" one of the other officers asked.

Bradham was still steaming and didn't want to talk to anybody else at the moment. "Yeah, yeah, let's hurry it up! I got somewhere I gotta go after here."

After putting his phone down, Charlotte looked at her boyfriend. Overhearing most of the conversation, she wasn't exactly thrilled.

"What?" Hall asked.

"We're going to visit Jernigan?"

"Oh. Well, like I told Bradham, that is the next step."

"If he just killed Guzman, you really think he's going to want to see us?"

"Probably not."

"So what are we gonna do?"

"I dunno. I guess we'll figure that out when we get there."

"That's not a plan," Charlotte said.

"Didn't say it was. Just said that's what I was gonna do."

"I don't like this, Brandon."

"I don't like it either. But we agreed to do this. And as long as we're on it, I'm gonna go where the clues lead me. And right now, it's leading to Jernigan."

"Is Bradham gonna meet us there or something?"

"I doubt it."

"Maybe we should just let the police take over."

"They're not taking over anything," Hall said. "And they won't unless we have more evidence. That's what they need. And that's what we're going to find. Evidence."

15

Hall and Charlotte were already in the car, driving to the address they had on Robbie Jernigan. Hall's phone rang, and as soon as he saw it was Bradham, braced himself for a lecture. He could have ignored the call, but it wasn't really Hall's style to block people out. He usually tried to meet things head on, no matter how big or small, or how important it was.

"Yeah?"

"Nice greeting," Bradham said.

"Sorry."

"Whatever. Anyway, you know those two guys you got picked up that were waiting for you outside the pharmacy Zeller worked at?"

"I'm not likely to forget."

"I just got word from the other detective that they

both have ties to Jerry Guzman. They all served time together. Probably have stayed in touch since."

"That kind of cinches is it, doesn't it?" Hall said. "If they were following me, and they're linked up with Guzman, who has the initials, that's gotta mean they were the ones in my apartment, doesn't it?"

"I would say that's probably a good chance. They haven't admitted to anything yet, but the other detective's gonna keep working on them. Maybe one of them will break."

"Thanks. Let me know, huh?"

"Yeah, I will. Sounds like you're in a car," Bradham said, hearing a horn blare. "I can hear the traffic."

"Maybe you should be a cop. You're observant."

"Yeah, real funny. Almost as funny as thinking you might be on your way to visit Jernigan, which I know you're not, right?"

"What? There's a lot of traffic; can't hear what you're saying."

"Brandon, listen to me, this guy is dangerous."

"Who's cantankerous?"

"Don't play games, I know full well you can hear me."

"Cheer who?"

Bradham sighed and shook his head, knowing he was wasting his breath. "You better be careful."

"About what?"

Bradham rolled his eyes and continued shaking his head. "Listen, I don't want to be called to another crime scene and have the body I'm looking at be you. Just be careful."

"I'll talk to you later."

As soon as Hall hung up, Charlotte started grilling him, overhearing part of his conversation.

"Who's linked up with Guzman?"

"The two guys that were following us and were waiting outside the pharmacy," Hall said. "They did time together."

"So that proves they were the ones?"

"Well, I don't know if it proves it, unless one of them talks and admits it. But it sure does make it likely."

It was another twenty minutes until they got to Jernigan's apartment. When they arrived, Charlotte couldn't have been less impressed. She parked, then sat there, looking at the building.

"Seriously?"

"What?" Hall asked.

"What is it with these guys and dirty, crummy apartments? Do they have something against living in nicer areas?"

Hall laughed. "Well, I imagine the rent is cheaper."

"It would have to be free for me to live here. And even that is pushing it. They'd probably have to pay me."

"Well, not everyone has the same standard of living as you."

"Same standard? You gotta have no standard to live

here. Looks like the whole building's about to fall down."

"I think you're pushing it a little with that one."

"Yeah, well, maybe."

"Could be that some of these guys aren't home often enough to really care," Hall said.

"I don't believe that for a second. You should still want a comfortable place to sleep. I'd be afraid once I closed my eyes that the ceiling would cave in on me."

"All right, now you're just getting ridiculous." Hall put his hand on the handle of the door and opened it slightly, alarming his girlfriend.

"What are you doing?"

Hall looked confused, not thinking it was a hard concept to understand. "Uh, getting out."

"Why?"

"To see Jernigan?"

"Why would you do that?"

"Did you forget why we're here?"

"I'm here 'cause you made me drive."

"I did not!" Hall replied. "You came of your own free will."

"Well, that was when I thought we were just gonna sit here and wait to see if he was here."

"We could be here for hours and not see anything."

"So? Isn't that part of the job? Waiting?"

Hall shrugged. "Probably. I'm not much on waiting though. I'd rather just get right to it."

"The man just beat you up, and you wanna get right back to him?"

"The man did not beat me up. He caught me with a sucker punch, then when I got the upper hand, his friend came to the rescue. For the record, I would have easily won."

"So you say. What if his friend is there too?"

"I dunno. We'll figure that out when we get there."

Charlotte sighed, then hung her head, not really wanting to move.

"You don't have to come," Hall said. "You can wait here until I get back."

"How many times do I have to tell you…"

"I know, I know, behind me. You know, I'm not really sure that strategy's been working too well."

"What do you mean?"

"Every time you're behind me it seems you get stuck in a fight and wind up with a few more bruises than you started with."

"Well, someone's gotta keep an eye on you."

Hall laughed. "Oh, is that what you're doing? Keeping an eye on me?"

"Yep."

"Oh, I see."

Hall then opened the door further and got out, drawing a look from Charlotte.

"We're really doing this?" she mumbled, low enough that Hall couldn't hear. Reluctantly, Charlotte also got out of the car. She stood in front of it and looked at the building. "I got a bad feeling about this."

"You always have a bad feeling about something."

"And wasn't I right the last time?"

"That really had no bearing on anything."

"Sometimes a girl just knows. Just stick with me a while and I'll teach you a few things."

Hall couldn't help but burst out laughing. "Oh, you will, huh?"

"Yep."

"Oh, OK. How about we go in instead of standing out here yapping?"

"Yeah, I guess, I mean, if you really want to get mixed up in another thing."

They walked into the front entrance of the building and started walking down the hallway to get to the elevator. Jernigan's place was on the fourth floor. Charlotte suddenly stopped and grabbed Hall's arm, squeezing it tightly. He put his hand on her grip, thinking he was about to lose feeling in his arm.

"Oh my God."

"What?" Hall asked, looking around. He didn't see a single other person there.

"I think I saw a rat."

Hall rolled his eyes and closed them. He peeled his girlfriend's fingers out of his skin. "Is that all?"

"What do you mean is that all? Those things are disgusting."

"Which way did it go?"

"I dunno, that way," Charlotte pointed. "Why?"

"You wanna go find it again and say hi?"

"Ew, that's gross."

"You know, some people have them as pets."

"That's just nasty."

They continued walking to the elevator, getting in and pushing the fourth-floor button.

"You know, I was thinking, maybe you should start carrying a gun."

"Why?" Hall asked.

"You may not have realized this, but we seem to have been getting into our fair share of trouble lately. And some of those people have guns. Might be a good idea. Just saying."

"Maybe. I have an idea too, though."

"What's that?"

"Why don't you start carrying a gun?"

"Seriously?" Charlotte replied. "You want me to do the shooting?"

"Well, I'd prefer that nobody has to do the shooting. That's why I'm not carrying one. I don't want to kill anybody. I did enough of that in the service."

"Yeah, well, normally I'd agree with that, but when people start shooting at us, I think it might be time."

"Nobody's shot at us."

"Not yet. Keep messing around with guys like this and I'm sure it'll happen sooner or later. With our luck, probably sooner."

"I think we'll be OK."

The elevator opened on the fourth floor, and Hall and Charlotte immediately locked eyes with a rough-looking gentleman who was standing there, waiting for the elevator himself. He was a middle-aged man, probably in his forties, maybe early fifties, balding head, scar on his cheek, and honestly looked like he needed a shower with what appeared to be dirt marks over his face and arms. Charlotte stood there paralyzed for a second, until she saw Hall getting off, walking past the man. She scurried off and grabbed hold of the back of his shirt as the man got on the elevator. Once they were a few feet away, Charlotte looked back and saw the elevator doors close with the man inside. Hall looked back at her and shook his head.

"Since when did you get so jumpy?"

"It's growing on me," Charlotte answered. "How would you like to be alone and run into that guy in a dark alley somewhere?"

"I'd rather not."

"Yeah, me too."

Hall continued walking as he looked for Jernigan's apartment. There were about forty apartments on each floor, so they walked the length of the hallway until they found the one they wanted.

"Here it is," Hall said.

"Looks like nobody's home."

Hall tilted his head and glared at his girlfriend. "Really?"

Charlotte shrugged. "Just taking a guess."

Hall curled his hand up into a fist and knocked on the door.

"Just for the record, I really hate this plan," Charlotte said.

"You already said it."

"Yeah, well, I'm saying it again."

Charlotte took a few steps back as she braced for anything to happen. Hall was more nonchalant, not really expecting anything in particular. Hall then knocked on the door again.

"See, told you. Nobody's home."

Hall knocked again. "Maybe he's napping."

"All the more reason we should stop. Most people are cranky if they're woken up from a nap."

Hall was not going to leave though. Not just yet. He kept on knocking, figuring someone had to answer, eventually.

"In all seriousness," Charlotte said, "the guy really might not be home."

"Maybe." Hall put his hand on the doorknob.

"What are you doing?"

"Seeing if it's locked."

"Why would you do that?"

"To see what's inside."

"This guy has a gun!"

Hall turned the knob of the door, and much to his surprise, it actually opened. He looked at Charlotte and smiled.

"See?"

"This is breaking and entering," Charlotte said.

"I'm not breaking anything. It's already open."

"Oh my gosh, we're gonna get arrested."

"We'll be fine." Hall opened the door further and was about to go inside. "C'mon."

Charlotte sighed. "This is not gonna end well."

16

Hall stepped foot in the apartment, somewhat apprehensively, almost expecting to get a greeting like the one he got in the last apartment he went in. Luckily, there were no fists flying at him this time. They did a quick look around the living room to see if anyone was there, but, thankfully, at least from Charlotte's point of view, they were alone.

"No mess on the floor," Charlotte said. "That's a good sign."

Hall took a quick peek in the kitchen. Since it was empty, they started checking out the rest of the place. It was only a one bedroom, one bath apartment, so there really wasn't a whole lot to check out, but Charlotte still had Guzman's apartment on her mind.

"Remember this is how the last one went. Body in the bedroom."

"We'll see," Hall said, undeterred.

Charlotte cautiously opened the bathroom as her boyfriend went through the other door. "Nothing here!"

Hall went inside the bedroom, looking around and under the bed, inside the closet, but there was no sign of Jernigan. He wasn't there. Charlotte came into the bedroom too, a little afraid of what she might see.

"He's not here," Hall said.

"That's a relief."

"It's not a relief. We can't get to the bottom of this unless we figure out how he fits into the puzzle."

"Maybe he doesn't. Maybe he's a square peg in a round hole."

"No, he fits. Somehow."

Hall started going through the dresser drawers.

"What are you doing?" Charlotte asked.

"As long as we're here we might as well see if we can find anything incriminating."

"I'm almost positive this is illegal."

"Well, then start looking too so we can get out of here."

"What am I looking for?"

"I dunno. Anything that might seem like it has to do with our case."

They went through the bedroom and closet, looking everywhere but not finding anything of interest. They did the same in the bathroom, also coming up empty. They then took to the living room and the kitchen. There was some mail on the kitchen counter that Hall picked up. It was mostly junk and a few bills. He didn't open them, but looked at the envelopes closely, turning them over just to make sure there was no writing on them. After inspecting each one, he tossed them back on the counter. Without finding anything in the first six pieces, Hall wasn't expecting to hit pay dirt on the remaining couple either, but the last one changed his mind. On the back was something scribbled down in black ink. It wasn't exactly the best penmanship. Hall held it up to the light to get a better look at it. It looked like some kind of address, though he couldn't really make it out. There was also a time on it. Nine o'clock.

"Charlotte, can you read this?"

Charlotte came in from the living room and took the envelope that Hall handed to her. "What's this?"

"I dunno. Looks like an address, but I can't make out what it says. Maybe you'll have better luck."

"Here, I'm an expert at reading chicken scratch."

"Is that so?"

"Yeah, a talent I've picked up over the years. Every guy I've ever been with has had poor handwriting. You learn to make things out."

"Oh, really? Every guy, huh? Sounds like a lot."

Charlotte took her eyes off the letter, realizing she'd made herself sound worse than she'd intended. "Well, I don't mean... not like I've been with a lot... I mean... let's just concentrate on this thing for now."

Hall smiled, thinking it was cute how she stammered like that when she got flustered. After a minute of analyzing the writing, Charlotte finally got a grasp of it.

"It says 2168 Cabots Road."

Hall looked at her for a second, then grabbed the envelope. He scrunched his face together as he tried to decipher the handwriting.

"How did you get that out of this?" Hall asked.

Charlotte grabbed the envelope again and started to point out her findings. "Look, it's right there in black and white. You can clearly see the numbers…"

"Numbers? Looks like a Z, then an l, maybe a zero, then I don't know what that last number is, then what looks like Carrots and a something else. You sure it's not a grocery list? Maybe he's shopping for vegetables."

"Please, it's really not all that hard if you just look closely. That Z is a two, the l is a one, you can see the line just barely come across to make that a six. There's clearly a line here separating this to make it an eight, and it's sloppily done, but the Carrots is definitely Cabots, and those last squiggly lines is an Rd. 2186 Cabots Road. Easy."

Hall picked up the letter again to try reading it, then looked at Charlotte again. He still wasn't seeing it, but he had to assume that she knew what she was talking about. She seemed confident. And since he couldn't make heads or tails out of it, that's what he was going to go with.

"I'll take your word for it."

"So what are we gonna do now?" Charlotte asked.

"We're gonna find out all we can about this address."

The two left the apartment, though they didn't have the intention of going home. That would just be wasted time. Charlotte had her laptop in the car, so they could find the nearest free Wi-Fi and hop on so they didn't have to lose time travelling. There was a fast-food restaurant a few blocks away, so they went there.

They took a booth and ate while they went on Charlotte's laptop. They checked public records first to find out what they could about the house. It was last sold five years ago, and upon seeing the street view of the house, they were convinced nobody was living there. It looked run-down.

"It might not still look like that," Hall said. "That image was taken three years ago, so it could've been cleaned up since then."

Charlotte continued typing away. "Says the owner is James Rankin."

"Rankin," Hall repeated, hoping that by saying the name, it would trigger some memory of it. Nothing came to him though. "Doesn't ring a bell. Can you do a search for him?"

"I can try."

Charlotte typed Rankin's name into the search engine. A lot of possibilities came up, but nothing that stood out. Without more to go on, it could have been just about anybody. She tried digging in to find a connection between Jernigan and Rankin, but there was nothing there. At least nothing that she could find. She was good, but they figured maybe they could use some extra help.

"Maybe if I call Bradham, he'll have something on this guy," Hall said.

Charlotte agreed, though she kept digging away herself, hoping to find something on her own. Hall called the detective, who picked up after five rings.

"Hey, nice to see you're still alive," Bradham said.

"Isn't it? Nice for us too."

"So what do you want? I imagine this isn't a social call just to say hello."

"Well, we swung by Jernigan's apartment. He wasn't there."

"Surprise, surprise. Better for you guys that he wasn't."

"Yeah, anyway, we found evidence that Jernigan is supposed to go to this address at nine o'clock tonight. Well, maybe tonight. It didn't say what day."

"What evidence?"

"Found an envelope with the address and time scribbled on the back."

"Found an envelope where?" Bradham asked, getting an idea of what the answer would be.

"Well,, you know that's not really important. What is important is that we found it."

"Brandon, did you break into this guy's apartment?"

"Absolutely not."

"Then how and where did you find this envelope? I'm sure it wasn't just lying in the hallway for anybody to find, was it?"

"There was a stack of mail in front of his apartment, and we just happened to pick it up."

"Just lying on the ground in front of his apartment, huh?"

"Yep."

"So it wasn't in a mailbox at the front of the building like everyone else's?"

"Apparently not," Hall replied. "Maybe he'd taken it from the box, went up to his apartment, got distracted by a phone call or something, dropped his mail, and then left? Who knows?"

"Brandon, you broke into this guy's apartment!"

"We did not!"

"Then how'd you get this envelope? Now tell me the truth or I'll come over there and book you right now on suspicion."

Hall sighed. "Fine, I'll tell you what happened."

"Oh, this should be good."

"We got there, went to knock on the door, saw that it was already open. So, being a good citizen, we decided to go in and see if there were any problems, you know, especially after seeing what happened to Guzman."

"Uh, huh."

"So we went through the place, saw that nobody was there, and we started to leave. As we were leaving, we saw some papers on the floor. I picked them up, which also had an envelope on it, and put them back on the table. I happened to glance at it and saw this address written down, figuring it might be important. That's all we did."

"How convenient for you... to just happen to find an envelope on the floor, facing the proper direction for you."

"Yeah, a bit of good luck, I suppose. Sometimes you just get a break."

"How fortunate."

"You really think I'd break into someone's apartment?"

"It crossed my mind."

"Well, I didn't. See what happens when you jump to conclusions?"

"Yeah, right. So what are you calling for?"

"I told you. We found an address. I assume that Jernigan had written it. Just wanted to see if you got anything on it."

"What, you haven't checked it out yet?"

"We checked public records," Hall answered. "Not much to it there. Nothing interesting."

Bradham sat down at his desk and went on his computer. "All right, give me the address?"

"It's 2186 Cabots Road."

"Doesn't sound familiar," Bradham said, typing the address in.

"It's apparently owned by a James Rankin."

Bradham stopped looking at his screen, not sure if he just heard right. "What'd you say?"

"I said it's owned by James Rankin. At least that's what public records say."

"Rankin, huh?"

"Yeah. Why, you know him?"

"I know of him."

"Who is he?"

"He's a ghost, a phantom."

"Say what?"

"He's a name that pops up every now and again, usually in regards to some type of crime that he's involved in."

"Now you know where he lives."

"Not that simple."

"What do you mean? Why not?"

"Because I'm sure he doesn't actually live there," Bradham replied.

"Why not? He owns it."

"He also owns half a dozen other places in the city. And he doesn't live in any of them. We think he just used them to conduct some of his business in. And that's the ones we know about. We suspect he's got a dozen more that we don't know about."

"I don't quite understand. If..."

"Listen, we believe that James Rankin is an alias for

some very intelligent criminal out there, who buys these distressed properties for a while, then cleans them up and sells them after he doesn't need them anymore."

"That still doesn't make any sense," Hall said. "If you know this guy's a criminal, and you can check when he buys a house, or when he sells a house, there's real estate agents involved, there's…"

"I'll just stop you right there. It's not that simple. Every real estate agent we've checked with about James Rankin describes a completely different guy. Sometimes he's white, sometimes he's black, sometimes he's Asian, sometimes he's Middle Eastern, curly hair, bald, crew cut, beard, mustache, goatee, clean shaven, tall, short, fat, thin, athletic, young, old, middle-aged… as you can see, every description of James Rankin leads you nowhere."

"But if you know when he buys a house, eventually the real guy is going to come around."

"You would think, wouldn't you?" Bradham said. "Doesn't work out that way though. For instance, I can tell you for a fact that we've sat outside five of his properties that he recently acquired, staked out these places for weeks… and nothing. Not a single person showed up. This guy's not dumb. He buys these places, sits on them for a while until he knows we're no longer watching, then does what he does with them."

"What about these imposters that he uses?"

"Yeah, we've talked to most of them. None of them

know what's going on. They're all approached by a different guy, again, none of whom look alike, and are given some money to do the deal for him. They couldn't pick out the real James Rankin if they were standing next to him."

"What do you think this guy does with these places?" Hall asked.

"Who knows? Could be anything. Drugs, guns, money, prostitution, maybe all of it. Your guess is as good as mine."

"How long's he hold these properties for?"

"There's no specific time. You think this guy's gonna be dumb enough to hold everything for exactly six months or a year? Sometimes three months, sometimes six, a year. There was one property we discovered that he held for five years."

"And you have no idea the real identity of this guy?"

"Nope. I mean, there's ideas floated around from time to time, but nothing that can ever be proven or anything that sticks."

"How long have you known about this guy?"

"First time we heard his name was about three years ago, and he's been a thorn in our side ever since. Problem is that we're never out in front of him. Anytime we see his name, it's something that's already happened days or weeks before, so by the time we get involved, he's already gone."

"Sounds like a tricky guy."

"Yeah, question is, what's he doing involved with Jernigan?"

"And Zeller and Guzman."

"You're still taking a leap with that," Bradham said. "Even if you're right with everything, and Jernigan was involved with Guzman and Zeller, that doesn't automatically link Rankin in too. They could have completely unrelated business. A plus B does not always equal C."

"Yeah, you're right. It would be nice if it all tied in though."

"A lot of things would be nice. Doesn't make it so."

"Hey, what if Jernigan is actually Rankin?"

"You really think he would need to write down the address of a place he already owns? Don't you think he would know it already?"

"Yeah, didn't think of that."

"When did you say this thing was happening?"

"Don't know," Hall answered. "There was just a time, no date. Nine o'clock. Why? Can you spare somebody?"

"For what?"

"A stakeout."

"Are you kidding? You don't even know what day it is. It could've already happened. It could've went down yesterday for all you know."

"Or it could be happening tonight."

"Listen, I don't have men to spare right now unless

I know for sure something's going down. We're spread too thin already."

"It's fine. Charlotte and I will go there and see what happens."

Hall could hear the sigh through the phone. "You're really starting to get knee deep in this."

"I think so too."

"You need to be careful about the people you're dealing with now. You're not talking about what happened to a college kid, now you're talking about dealing with some real bad people who will have no second thoughts about taking you out."

"I can handle myself," Hall said.

"I know you can. But I'm not talking about all your Bruce Lee stuff. All your karate and jujitsu and all that stuff won't make much difference with a guy who pulls a gun on you and pulls the trigger before you get your hands and feet flying."

"I'll be careful."

"So you say. You might wanna start thinking about carrying a gun with you. Legally."

"You know, Charlotte said the same thing."

"She's a smart woman, maybe you should try listening to her sometime."

"Listening to her is how I got into this to begin with."

"OK, well, Jernigan's known to be a violent guy. And who knows who or what Rankin is, or what they've got planned, or how many other bad people will be around, so you need to be careful."

"You keep saying that," Hall said. "I know. I will."

"All right. Well, good luck. And I'll try to see if I can get a few things done or moved around and send one or two people your way, just so you got some extra protection."

"Thanks. I'd appreciate that."

"Yeah, well, don't thank me yet."

After they got off the phone, Charlotte was curious about the parts of the conversation she heard.

"What was that all about?"

Hall then repeated what he was told about James Rankin.

"This whole thing is getting weirder by the minute," Charlotte said. "I mean, how did we get here?"

Hall looked down at the table and shook his head. "I don't know."

"How does Jernigan and Rankin fit in all of this?"

"I don't know. I guess we're about to find out."

17

After eating, Hall and Charlotte drove over to the address they found in Jernigan's apartment. They got there a full hour before the time listed on the envelope, wanting to be there in plenty of time to see if there was any activity before the supposed meeting was to take place.

"What are we gonna do if no one shows up?" Charlotte asked.

"I don't know."

"I mean, Bradham's right, there's no guarantee it's gonna be tonight. Could've been yesterday, last week, or maybe even next week."

"I dunno, I just feel like that had to be done today," Hall said. "If it was old mail, he'd have thrown it out, wouldn't he?"

"Maybe."

"And if the meeting was last week, he wouldn't have kept the address just lying around, would he?"

"Probably not."

"So my own deductive reasoning tells me that since there was no date on it to indicate a future time, and it's not likely it already happened, that logically tells me it's tonight."

"For some strange reason that actually makes sense to me."

Hall laughed. "What are you saying? I don't usually make sense?"

"Well…"

They sat across the street from the address they were staking out. It was a corner residential property that was in desperate need of repairs. It was a ranch-style house that needed a new roof, new windows, paint, not to mention all the work needed inside.

"Why do all these guys do business or live in stuff that makes your skin crawl?" Charlotte asked. "Wouldn't they prefer nicer surroundings?"

"I guess the theory is that other people like nicer surroundings too. You know, witnesses, onlookers, nosey busybodies, people like that. I guess they figure they don't have to worry about that with messy or broken-down stuff. Nobody's likely to come wandering around places like this unless they have business there."

"I suppose so. What are we gonna do if a bunch of

people actually show up? You can't go in there if, like, ten people go in."

"I don't know. We can take pictures, get license plate numbers, try to figure things out. We'll have to see how it goes."

They sat there for the next hour, keeping their eyes peeled for any visitors. No one showed up yet though. That included any police help that they weren't really expecting, anyway.

"Guess Bradham couldn't get anyone freed up," Charlotte said.

"Wasn't really counting on it, anyway."

"No. Still would've been nice though."

"It would've, but the only people we can count on in this is us."

"What do you really think happened with Keith?"

"I don't know," Hall replied. "My guess is that he somehow got mixed up with some really bad people and got in way over his head."

"Maybe. Or maybe it wasn't something he did. Maybe it was something he saw. Maybe he witnessed something he wasn't supposed to."

"Could be."

"I just have a hard time believing he would intentionally get involved with people like Jernigan, Rankin, people like that."

"Yeah, well, we didn't actually know him, did we?"

"You're always more skeptical."

"It's served me well over the years."

A couple minutes before nine, they slunk down into their seats as a car drove past them and stopped in front of the distressed property they were looking at. Whoever was inside the car sat there for a few minutes without getting out.

"Who's that?" Charlotte asked.

"Can't tell. Can't get a shot of the license plate from here either."

Three minutes later, a shadowy figure emerged from the car, looking around before heading into the house.

"That kind of looks like Jernigan, doesn't it?" Charlotte said.

"Yeah, it does."

"Well, half the meeting's complete. Now we just gotta wait and see who he's waiting for."

"You know what? We should probably let Bradham know the meeting's going down now. Maybe he can get people here in time."

"What if they get here before whoever Jernigan's meeting? That'll blow it."

"But if we don't call, these guys will leave and who knows if we'll run into them again," Hall replied.

Hall pulled out his phone and called the detective, who was still catching up on paperwork back in his office.

"Steve? Looks like we hit pay dirt. We're outside that address right now, and it looks like Jernigan just showed up."

"Really? Anyone else there?"

"Not yet as far as we can tell."

"All right, you guys stay put and don't approach the house or anything. I'll get a few guys together and be right over."

"How long's that gonna take?"

"Probably about twenty minutes to get there," Bradham answered.

"OK. See you when you get here." Hall then looked at Charlotte. "He's on his way."

Ten minutes passed and there was still no sign of whoever Jernigan was supposed to be meeting. Hall was starting to get a little antsy.

"I'm not liking this," Hall said.

"It's only ten minutes. They could still be here."

"I'm not sure about that. Guys like this don't generally like people being late. Usually means something's wrong."

"Could be anything," Charlotte said. "Doesn't mean something's wrong."

Hall continued looking at the house, another thought coming to him. "Either that or the person's already inside."

"What? How could they be inside? We've been watching this place for over an hour. We would've seen someone else going in."

"Not if they were on foot coming from the opposite direction and cutting through the neighbors' yards."

"I kind of doubt someone would go to that trouble. What would be the point?"

"The point would be if they thought the place was being watched, they could slip in undetected."

"But if something went wrong, and they had to escape quickly, there's no getaway car or anything."

"Who needs a getaway car if you can disappear?" Hall said, thinking of Rankin's propensity of vanishing.

"I dunno, I would think we would actually see someone else going in."

"Why? What else with this case leads you to believe that we're going to get what's expected? We haven't gotten that yet."

"There's always a first time."

"Not when dealing with these people. They always stick to the same methods. It's just what they do."

"Why would they assume the house is being watched?" Charlotte asked.

"Maybe they're getting paranoid. Maybe they're thinking everything's falling apart so it's good sense to take precautions."

"You know, I've been thinking, maybe we got this wrong."

"How so?"

"Well, we've been thinking that Guzman killed Keith, right? And then Jernigan killed Guzman to cover it up," Charlotte said.

"Yeah?"

"What if Jernigan killed Keith too? Somehow

Guzman found out about it, or knew about it, and tried to stop it, and they killed him to silence him?"

"Makes sense except for the fact that Guzman and his two friends jumped us in our apartment," Hall replied. "I kind of doubt an innocent man would do something like that."

"Maybe he was trying to warn us to stay off the case?"

"If so, I think that's taking things to extremes. You could always just send a postcard."

"Just a thought."

"And if we didn't already know those other two clowns following us were tied in with Guzman, I'd probably say it might be more plausible. Plus, if Guzman was innocent and knew something happened with Keith, why not take it to the cops? Sitting on it wouldn't make much sense to me."

"Some people are more afraid of the police than the alternative."

"Well, the alternative got him killed."

They waited another five minutes. There was still no sign of anyone else. Hall was getting antsy.

"This isn't right."

"Relax," Charlotte said.

"No. There's no way a guy like Jernigan, who's hot, who just killed someone, would just be sitting in this place for fifteen minutes waiting for someone. He wouldn't take the chance. Men like him, they're in and out. They're afraid to stay in one spot for too long."

"Maybe the person he's waiting for is really important and he's got no choice?"

Hall wasn't buying it. "No. I don't care if he was waiting for the president. He wouldn't wait this long." Hall slipped his fingers inside the handle of the door and opened it an inch.

"What are you doing?"

"I'm moving in closer."

"What? No!"

"I gotta see what's going on in there."

"Brandon, the police should be here in five minutes. Just wait."

"What if they're late?"

"You know, for someone who wasn't all that eager to get involved in all this stuff, you sure like to charge into things."

"If I'm gonna do something, I'm gonna go all-out," Hall replied. "If you're not all-in, might as well stay home, right?"

Charlotte sighed. "Just wait for the police to get here."

"I'll be fine."

Hall opened the door all the way and got out of the car much to Charlotte's displeasure. Hall ran across the street, in the direction of another house, just in case anyone inside the house Jernigan was in was watching. Hall stood against the side of the house directly across from the house he was watching, taking everything in as he waited for the right moment to move closer. After about a minute, Hall ran across the street, taking cover behind the car that Jernigan drove up in. He pulled on the handle of the door, but it was locked. Hall, while still ducking, moved around to the back of the vehicle and took a picture of the license plate so that he could run it later.

Hall stayed in his spot for a minute, still keeping his eyes focused on the house. He didn't hear or see anything out of the ordinary. He didn't hear voices, didn't see shadows moving past the windows. Nothing. It was much too quiet for his liking. He knew something wasn't right. He was just about to move closer to the house when suddenly a shot rang out. Hall flinched, not expecting to hear the sound of gunfire. It came from inside the house. Then there was another shot. Hall instinctively looked back at Charlotte's car and saw her getting out, standing by the door, looking at him. He put his hand up, not wanting her to move any closer. He wasn't staying put though.

Hall quickly ran to the front door and tried to pull on it, but it was locked. The door looked like the sturdiest piece of the house, so he didn't want to spend too long trying to break through it. Instead, he ran around to the back of the house, hoping there was an easier entrance point. He was right. The back of the house had a sliding glass door that looked like it had already been broken into a time or two. There were several holes in the glass, including one by the lock. Hall tried to open it the easy way, but it was locked. He stuck his hand in the hole and then unlocked it, sliding it open.

The house was dark, but Hall still stepped inside, keeping his eyes open and staying alert for anything. He assumed something would jump out at him at some point. Considering he'd heard gunshots, he started looking around the room, assuming he would find a body, whether that person was dead or just badly injured. Of course, the shots could have missed their intended target, but considering there were no other shots fired, Hall assumed they hit what they were aiming at.

Hall thought he was in some kind of family room or bonus room. Since he didn't see anything there, he moved into what was the kitchen, though it looked like rats and mice were probably the only things eating anything in there lately. Hall then moved into the living room, where he thought he noticed a large object in the middle of the floor. It was dark, and he couldn't make it out from his position, so it could have been a body. It also could have been a bunch of debris or trash thrown about.

Hall stayed in his spot for a few moments, to make sure he wasn't walking into anything nefarious. After thinking it was safe, he took a few steps forward. He was suddenly taken by surprise from behind, getting knocked in the back of the head with something big and heavy. Hall went down to the floor, holding the back of his head, as he looked up and saw someone standing over top of him. Hall couldn't see his face in the darkness, plus the man was wearing some kind of hat that was pulled down low.

Before the man was able to do anything else, Hall stuck his legs out and tripped the man up, sending him to the ground as well. Hall quickly got back to his feet and jumped on top of the man, the two of them wrestling around as they both tried to get the upper hand. Neither of them did though. Sirens started to wail in the distance. The police were closing in. The stranger knew that meant he had no more time to waste and had to leave now. He didn't have time to deal with Hall. The man was able to push Hall off him, then stood up. Hall did the same, blocking his exit path through the back door. The man reached his hand around to his back and brought out what appeared to be a gun. He pointed it at Hall. Hall put his hands up and hoped the man wouldn't fire. Instead, the man lunged forward, touching Hall's chest with the device. Instant pain went through Hall's body and he dropped to the ground.

With Hall now down and incapacitated, the stranger ran out of the room and out the back door, going out the way he came in. Hall struggled to move for the next several minutes as police started to make their way inside the building. Hall could hear a bunch of noises and people talking, though he still had trouble moving. It was almost like he was paralyzed.

After a few more minutes, Hall was able to move

his arms and legs a bit more. The pain started to subside a little. The police came into the room, shining their bright flashlights all over the place. Hall let out a groan as an officer came over to him.

"Got one here!" the officer shouted.

Bradham was one of the men who came over to check. "That's Hall. You OK?" Bradham knew he was hurt but didn't want to move him yet until he knew what the problem was.

Hall continued moving his arms and legs around, almost feeling like they were back to normal. "Yeah, I think so."

"What's the matter? You hit somewhere?"

Hall put his hand on his chest and started rubbing it. "No. I feel like I got shocked or something. Then everything went numb."

"Probably got hit with a taser or some type of stun gun."

Hall opened his eyes wide and blinked fast as he tried to regain clarity in his mind. "Wow. I don't think I've felt something like that since my training days with the Rangers."

"Who was it that got you?"

Hall was finally able to sit up as he took a few deep breaths. "I don't know. It was dark. Couldn't see his face."

"What are you doing in here, anyway? Why didn't you wait for us?"

"I was outside, heard two shots, didn't want someone to get away before you got here."

"Well, you sure paid the price for that decision."

"Tell me about it." Hall held the back of his head. "He nailed me with something else first too." He then took his hand away and held it in front of him to see if there was any blood. Luckily there wasn't. He then thought about the shots he heard. "You find anyone else in here?"

"Yeah," Bradham answered. "Jernigan."

Hall was almost afraid to ask the next question. "Dead?"

"As a doornail. Two in his chest."

Hall looked disappointed, feeling like they'd lost a big piece of evidence. "Don't suppose you found the guy who clobbered me, huh?"

"No, he's long gone. I got a patrol car cruising the neighborhood, but the likelihood of them finding the guy is practically nothing." Bradham then turned to one of the uniformed officers. "Hey, go outside and tell the woman that he's all right."

"Can't you just let her come in?" Hall asked.

"Wish I could, but this is a crime scene now. Can't have anyone else coming in and possibly contaminating anything."

"You really think you're gonna get anything out of here except a handful of dust?"

"Probably not. Procedure is procedure though. Gotta do it by the book."

"Yeah, I know. Hey, you don't think the guy that walloped me was actually Rankin, do you?"

Bradham shrugged. "Who knows? I guess it's possible. Equally possible it's someone he hired to do it. It's also possible it was Jernigan's partner, you know, the guy who was with him at Guzman's place. Still haven't located or identified him yet."

"Partners turning on each other?"

"It's happened before."

"I know. I just wish we had more answers here."

"You and me both, pal. You and me both."

"Seems the further we get into this thing the more confusing it's getting," Hall said.

"Yeah. And it's not likely gonna get any easier from here either."

Hall went outside the house to get checked out by the paramedics. He felt fine, other than being a little sore, and declined going to the hospital for further testing. After the paramedics were done with him, Hall walked over to where Charlotte was standing and put his arms around her.

"You scared me for a second."

"I'm fine," Hall replied.

"It could've turned out a lot different."

"But it didn't. All that matters now is that I'm here."

"It was an unnecessary chance you took. You didn't need to go in there with the police on the way."

Hall felt like he couldn't really debate the point. "You're right. I should've waited."

"I think we should call it a night and go home," Charlotte said. "Can't really do anything else tonight."

"Won't get an argument from me."

"Maybe if you're good on the way, I'll give you a massage when we get home."

Hall smiled. "Sounds like an offer I couldn't refuse."

18

After getting his massage, Hall fell asleep on Charlotte's couch. He woke up the next morning to a pleasant smell: Charlotte making breakfast. She was a great cook. Hall thought she could probably make just about anything she wanted. He walked into the kitchen and saw Charlotte's back was turned toward him as she was standing over the stove. He snuck up behind her and put his arms around her waist and kissed her neck. She then turned her head around to kiss him on the lips.

"Good morning," she said. "This is a nice way to start the day."

"I certainly wouldn't complain about starting every day like this."

Charlotte smiled and gave him another kiss. "Sit down and eat your breakfast."

"Smells really good." Hall kissed her lips. "I meant both you and the food. You more."

"Smooth talker."

"You ever thought about becoming a chef? You could probably get your own television show and become a big star."

Charlotte rolled her eyes, feeling like he was feeding her some ridiculous line. "I think you need to be tall, pretty, talk well in front of people, and a lot of other things for that to happen."

Hall took a step back as he looked her over. He then moved in closer again, holding her in his arms. "Well, you got the most important thing going for you out of those things."

"Oh, yeah? What's that?"

"You're as pretty as can be."

They passionately kissed, only stopping when Charlotte smelled something burning.

"Oh my gosh!" Charlotte yelled, quickly turning around and turning the stove off. She took the pan off the stove and grabbed a plate. "I think I saved it in time."

Hall laughed. "Even if you didn't, it's no big deal."

After Charlotte finished what she was doing, she turned back around to her boyfriend, putting her hands on his chest. "Are you feeling OK?"

"Yeah, I'm good. Your massage and a good night's rest did the trick."

"Probably more so the rest."

"I'll lean more towards your massage as the tipping point. Is there anything you can't do well?"

"Apparently the only thing I can't do is hold you back."

Hall sat down and looked at the table, sorry for making her worry like that. "I'm sorry. I promise I'll try not to do that again."

They ate and continued to talk about the events of the previous night.

"Who do you think that was last night?" Charlotte asked.

Hall took a sip of his orange juice before responding. "I dunno. I feel like maybe it was Rankin. I don't know why though, just a gut feeling, I guess. It really could have been anybody."

"Could've been Jernigan's partner. You know, the one at Guzman's apartment."

"Could be, I guess."

"What if they're the same guy? Rankin and the guy at Guzman's apartment with Jernigan?"

"We can't really dismiss anything at this point."

"I think that's probably where we need to go next," Charlotte said. "Find out who that guy was with Jernigan."

Hall nodded, agreeing completely. "Yeah, there's no point right now in trying to find Rankin. Police have been doing that for the last couple years. I doubt we'd have more luck than they do in a couple days."

"Where are we gonna start? Feels like we kinda hit a dead end."

Hall shook his head. "No, we didn't hit a dead end. We just have to go down a side road. You're right, though, finding whoever was with Jernigan in Guzman's apartment will be key. He likely knows what's going on with everything."

"There's going to be a problem with that, I think."

"What's that?"

"If whoever this guy is learns of what happened to Jernigan, he's probably going to dig a hole so far down you won't be able to find him. He's going to be afraid of the same thing happening to him."

"Yeah, I know," Hall replied.

"Maybe after breakfast we should go see Bradham, look at all the known associates of Jernigan. Maybe if we see a few faces, we can pick the guy out."

"Yeah, I think that's as good a plan as any right now."

As soon as the pair finished eating and cleaned up, they scooted out of the apartment and went down to the police station. On the way there, Hall, sitting in the passenger seat again, kept looking in the mirror. Ever since he noticed that blue car following them, he'd been on the lookout for others. Luckily, he didn't see anyone else doing the same this time.

Hall and Charlotte had been to the station so often lately that people were beginning to recognize them. They went by Bradham's office, but he wasn't there.

They then started walking through the building—at least the parts they had access to—and eventually found the detective sitting at a table in the cafeteria. Bradham was just sitting there, a bunch of papers and folders on the table in front of him, and a white Styrofoam cup in hand. Bradham was focused on his work and didn't notice the pair walking toward him until they sat down across from him. Bradham sighed, wondering what the issue was now.

"Oh, man, you guys again?"

Hall smiled. "Glad to see us, huh?"

"You know, you're here so much people are beginning to think you work here."

"Well, we're all after the same thing, right? Justice?"

"Yeah, I suppose so."

"Little early for lunch, isn't it?"

"I'm not eating," Bradham answered. "Sometimes I like to come down here in the mornings, have a coffee, do some work. It's kind of quiet at this time. Can think to myself without having to worry about checking emails or phones ringing."

"Makes sense."

"So how you feeling today? A little less shocked?"

Hall tilted his head and gave a crooked smile, not believing Bradham had come up with a joke like that. "Really?"

Bradham laughed. "Sorry, couldn't resist."

"I'm sure."

"So what are you two here for?"

"Jernigan's partner," Charlotte replied. "Right now, we figure he's the key that can tell us what's going on."

"You think so?"

"Well, if he was with Jernigan at Guzman's, then he should be able to tell us why, which should lead back to Zeller, don't you think?"

"Possibly. You know who it is?"

"No," Hall said. "That's why we're here."

"Let me guess. You want me to go through the files and dig up any known associates."

"That's pretty much it."

"Maybe I should just give you a key to my office. Then you can go in anytime you like or when you need something."

"Well, that would be more convenient."

Bradham rolled his eyes. He took one last sip of his coffee, got up and threw the empty cup in a trash can. He grabbed his papers and folders and started walking. "All right, let's go."

Hall and Charlotte got up, following the detective back to his office. Once they got there, Bradham unlocked the door and immediately went over to his desk. Hall and Charlotte took seats across from him. Bradham started typing on his computer.

"You know, whoever this guy is, if he knows Jernigan's dead, he might be on the lam."

"We came to the same conclusion," Hall said. "Especially if he knows or is tied in with Rankin somehow."

"Or he might not know him at all."

"Possible. But at this point it seems like everything's intertwined, doesn't it?"

"Not necessarily. Jernigan and Rankin—assuming he was the one who killed him—could have had completely unrelated business. Jernigan was sort of a freelancer and had his hand in a lot of things; could have been any of them that got him killed."

Hall sighed, knowing it was possible. "Yeah, could be. Just seems a bit too coincidental to me, don't you think? I mean, Zeller leads us to Guzman, who is then killed by Jernigan, who is then killed by whoever that was, possibly Rankin."

"And as I've told you before, two plus two doesn't always equal four."

"Well, let's just say that there is a connection and the numbers do work out..."

Bradham interrupted him, already knowing what he was going to say. "You're assuming that Zeller was actually killed by Guzman, right? That's what you're thinking?"

"Yeah, I'd say that's the prevailing theory."

"And you're also thinking that Rankin hired Jernigan to kill Guzman to prevent him from talking?"

"Bang on so far."

"And now you're thinking that Jernigan was killed to prevent the link being established to Guzman?"

"You got it."

"So what you're saying is this all comes back to Rankin."

"Definitely crossed my mind," Hall said.

"So Rankin was mixed up with Zeller somehow, and for whatever reason that went sideways, then he hired Guzman to kill Zeller and make it look like he overdoses? Then Rankin hears you get involved and starts asking questions, so he sends Guzman and his goons to rough you up? That doesn't work, so he just decides to cut bait and eliminate the problem by killing Guzman?"

"That's what I'm thinking."

"And then you're saying that Rankin hears about your involvement with Jernigan, maybe you can identify him and tie him back to this whole mess, and to prevent that, Rankin cuts bait again and kills this guy too."

"You said it all perfectly."

"Yeah, I thought so," Bradham said. "There's a whole lot in there that needs to be sorted out."

"Maybe so. But can you deny that it makes sense?"

"That's the problem. It doesn't make sense. While your theory, in theory, is sound, what doesn't add up is how a big-time criminal like Rankin would be involved with a college kid like Zeller. Where's the connection there?"

Hall sighed and rubbed his face. It was a legitimate question and one that he didn't have an answer to.

After a moment of thought, he ran his hand over his hair and scratched the top of his head.

"I dunno. There's gotta be something, doesn't there? Maybe Rankin hired Zeller to do something small and simple for him like drop off a package or something? Maybe somehow it went sideways, I don't know."

"I know this isn't what you wanna hear, but maybe it isn't connected," Bradham said. "Maybe you're right about Zeller. Maybe he didn't overdose himself. But maybe it was Guzman. They had some beef or whatever that led up to that result. But Guzman's also into a bunch of other things, one of those being something that leads to a visit from Jernigan, completely unrelated to Zeller. Whatever happens there happens, then Jernigan goes to that house to talk to Rankin, possibly about Guzman, or possibly something else unrelated, then he gets knocked off. Now isn't all that equally possible?"

Hall sighed and made a face, not wanting to admit that the detective could have been right. Eventually he had to though. "Yeah, I guess you're right. Possibly."

"I rest my case, your honor."

"But you also have to admit my theory holds water too."

"Find the link."

"Well, let's take a look at those pictures so we can find Jernigan's partner," Hall said. "Then we might have gotten it."

19

Bradham pulled up a list of Jernigan's known associates. It was actually a pretty lengthy list. Having been at it for over twenty years, including the time he spent in jail, Jernigan had made quite a few contacts. Bradham printed the list and handed it over to Hall to look over it. He passed it over to Charlotte.

"You probably got a better look at the guy than I did," Hall said.

"Yeah, most of that was on his back though."

"You think you're actually gonna be able to pick him out?" Bradham asked. "Like he said, you mostly got the wrong end of him."

"Yeah, but I still got a few glimpses of his face. Like after he threw me off and again when they ran out of the room. I still should be able to recognize him."

"And you didn't notice the guy?" Bradham asked, looking at Hall.

"Eh, not really. I was kind of busy at the time," Hall replied.

It didn't take Charlotte more than a couple minutes before she found him. She put the paper down on the desk and pointed to his picture. "This is the guy."

Bradham leaned forward and looked at it. "You're sure?"

"Positive. That's him."

"Who is he?" Hall asked.

"His name is Ferguson Ellis," Bradham replied.

"You know him?"

"I've had the pleasure of meeting him once. It was an unrelated case that it turned out he wasn't involved in. He was one of the suspects at the time."

"What are the chances he's still at this address?"

Bradham snickered. "Probably about five percent."

"Wow. You give better odds than I do. I was gonna say one."

"And I don't want you going over there and talking to him. I'll send someone over and see if he's there."

"Kind of hard to go over there and talk to a ghost. You know, considering he won't be there and all."

Bradham smiled. "I got the reference."

"Hey, you don't think Ellis might actually be Rankin, do you?"

Bradham shook his head, instantly nixing that thought. "No way. This guy is no criminal mastermind, believe me. He has his talents, but they're extremely limited."

"What exactly are his talents?" Charlotte asked.

"He's good at providing some extra muscle."

"That's it?"

"That's it. He packs a powerful punch in that small frame of his. He's only about five-four, five-five, but he's built like an ox. Obviously spends a lot of time working out. But that's where his value ends. If you need some extra muscle behind you, he's your guy. But he ain't the brightest fish in the barrel."

"I don't think that's the saying," Hall said.

"Yeah, I don't care."

"So what do we do now?"

"I'll tell you what you can do," the detective said. "Go home. We'll see if we can grab Ellis. We'll pick him up, we'll talk to him, and we'll see where that takes us."

"You can't just shuffle us off like that."

"Why not?"

"Because we're in this case as much as you are. You wouldn't even have this much if it wasn't for us."

"I won't dispute that. But now it's time for us to take over. As far as I can see, you've hit a wall, anyway."

"We'll just see about that. What about Guzman's buddies? The ones who were waiting for us outside the pharmacy. You ever get anything from them?"

"Nope. They admit to nothing. They say they don't know anything. All they'll admit to is waiting for you outside the pharmacy. They say Guzman asked them to keep an eye on you, but he didn't tell them why."

"That's a load of crap," Hall said. "Who follows people without getting a reason why?"

"Yeah, well, that's their story and they're sticking to it."

Charlotte started pulling on her boyfriend's arm. "C'mon, let's go."

"What? Why?"

"Steve's right; there's nothing else we can do here. Let's just go home."

Hall looked at her strangely, thinking this was an unusual move from her. "Really?"

"Yeah, let's go. If Ellis is at his address, then they'll pick him up and talk to him. And if he's not, there's nothing we can do there, anyway."

Bradham smiled, getting a smug look on his face, happy that someone was agreeing with him. "Finally, someone who gets it. She's a smart woman, Brandon. You'll be lucky to hang on to her. Maybe she'll rub off on you sometime."

Hall just looked at him and nodded. He really couldn't disagree that Charlotte was smart, or that he'd be lucky to hold on to her. It was just better to say nothing.

Before leaving, Charlotte grabbed the printout with Ellis' picture on it. "Can we take this?"

Bradham knew he shouldn't, but reluctantly agreed. "Yeah, go ahead."

"Thanks."

Hall and Charlotte got up and walked to the door to get ready to leave, but not before some final words from the detective.

"Remember, stay away from Ellis' place. I'm sending a car over there now, OK?"

"OK," Hall answered. "You let me know if you find anything?"

"Yeah, I guess I can do that."

"Thanks."

Hall and Charlotte left the office and walked out of the police station. Once back in their car, Hall had a few questions.

"Why'd you get us out of there so quickly? I probably could've worn him down a little more."

"Yeah, maybe," Charlotte said. "It wasn't getting us anywhere though. I mean, we all know Ellis isn't going to be at that address. If he is, then he's stupider than any of us give him credit for. Let the police go that way, we'll go ours."

"And which way is that?"

"Well, we got pictures of Ellis, Jernigan, and Guzman. Let's show them around to the people who knew Keith, see what we come up with. Maybe one of them saw one of these guys hanging outside his apartment or work or something."

Hall leaned over and kissed his girlfriend on the cheek. "Smart. Beautiful and smart."

"You expect anything less?"

"No."

They first went back to Zeller's apartment, luckily finding both his roommates there at the same time. Hall and Charlotte showed them pictures of everyone, but Guzman was the only one they recognized, and that was only because he worked at the pizza shop. They never saw Zeller and Guzman together anywhere else. And they couldn't identify the other two. After leaving the apartment, they went back to the pizza shop, wanting to talk to the ever-cooperative owner again. Just before walking in, Charlotte grabbed Hall's arm.

"You know he's gonna make us order pizza again."

Hall laughed. "Yeah."

"I'm almost pizza'd out."

"Nonsense. That's not even a thing."

"Of course it is."

"No, it's not. Who gets tired of pizza?"

"Umm, me!"

"That's ridiculous," Hall said. "Nobody gets tired of pizza. I could have pizza seven days a week."

"Well, that's just ridiculous. Nobody else would want to eat pizza seven days a week."

"I can't even believe we're having this conversation. Pizza is the premiere food. Never get tired of it."

"Yes, pizza is great, but not every single day."

They went inside and saw the owner by the counter, like usual. And just like the other times, they were made to order something before getting any information. They sat down at a booth as the owner got their order together.

"I told you," Charlotte said.

"So what? Their pizza's good."

"I should've ordered a sandwich instead."

"Stick with the pizza."

"Yeah, well, if we come here again, I'm not getting pizza next time. Maybe I'll get a salad instead."

Hall immediately scoffed at the idea. "Salad? Are you kidding?! Nobody goes to a pizza shop and gets a salad."

"Well, of course they do. If nobody got it, they wouldn't still offer it."

"Who goes to a pizza shop for a salad?"

"Uh, maybe people who are watching their weight?"

"So why would you come here?" Hall asked. "Why wouldn't you go to another place? One that's more conducive to that sort of thing. Nobody who's watching their weight goes to a pizza shop."

"You're so out of touch it's not even funny."

"I'm out of touch? You're out of touch. What are you gonna tell me next, that people have a salad and wash it down with some greasy fries? That's real healthy."

Charlotte rolled her eyes and shook her head. "You're lucky you're good-looking, because some of the views you have are just... ugh."

"Some of the views I have?! Really?"

A few minutes later, the owner came over with their usual order, pizza and a soda. As he sat down with them, eating himself, Charlotte wanted to make a point.

"Before we get into that, how are your salads here?"

"Our salads? Oh, they're fantastic. You should try one. I may be a bit biased, but they're very good."

Charlotte looked at Hall and smiled. "Really? Well, I'll have to try one next time."

"Oh, you will love it. I guarantee it."

"Does anybody come in here and just order a salad instead of pizza?"

"Oh, yes, all the time."

Charlotte glanced at Hall again, with a confident look on her face. "Is that so? Interesting."

"Yeah, some people come in here, trying to watch their weight, eat a little healthier, so we try to put a few healthy items on the menu."

"That's really interesting."

Hall sat there, listening to their exchange, knowing she was intentionally proving him wrong. He dug into his pizza until his girlfriend was done making fun of him. After several minutes, and done eating everything but the crust, they finally seemed to be finished.

"Are you done now?" Hall asked.

"What's the matter, dear? Did you not enjoy the conversation?"

"Now who's lucky they're good-looking?"

Charlotte smiled, not minding a little ribbing. "Yeah, I think I'm done now."

"Great. So can we get on with things?"

"Sure. Go right ahead."

"Thank you so much."

They both gave each other little fake smiles before moving on. Hall ate the rest of his crust and took a sip of his soda before turning his attention to the owner of the place. Hall took out the pictures of Jernigan and Ellis and turned them around, placing them down in front of the owner so he could take a good look at them.

"Have you ever seen these guys before?"

The owner leaned forward and looked down at them to get a better look. He picked the pictures up and held them closer to his face to inspect them a little more.

"Anything?" Hall asked. "Inside, outside, anywhere?"

"I don't know. I mean, they look familiar, but I can't say for sure. Maybe they were here, maybe not. It's tough to say."

"What about the guy who was outside arguing with Guzman?" Charlotte asked. "Was it either of these guys?"

The owner rubbed his chin as he thought. "No, I don't think so. These guys both look older. The guy that was arguing with Jerry was a younger kid, probably in his mid-twenties or so. These guys here are what, forty, forty-five, something like that?"

"That's about right," Hall replied.

"Yeah, neither of these guys are the ones. Sorry about that."

"It's all right." Hall then smiled. "At least we got a pizza out of it, huh?"

Done with the questioning, the owner then went back to his business as Hall and Charlotte finished their meal.

"We got ten pounds of air," Charlotte said.

"Not yet."

"What do you mean?"

"Well, we still have one person to go."

"You mean, what's her name, Sharon?"

Hall nodded. "Yeah."

Charlotte grunted, already not looking forward to the exchange. "Ugh, that'll be fun. She's always so happy to see us."

"Hey, last time we went there, something good came out of it."

"We almost got jumped."

"Yeah, but we turned it around, they went to jail, and we found out they were working with Guzman."

"I'd rather not go through all that again. I'd settle for something easier and simpler this time."

"Beggars can't be choosers."

20

After leaving the pizza shop, Hall and Charlotte went back to the pharmacy to have another talk with Sharon. They hoped she would be able to identify one of the men. Along the way, they started talking about the case, trying to make heads or tails of it.

"What do you think this whole thing's about?" Charlotte asked.

"I wish I knew."

"It's gotta be some type of mix-up or something, don't you think?"

"Mix-up how?"

"Like maybe they were after someone else and they got him mixed up with Keith or something like that."

Hall shook his head. "No, I don't think so."

"Why not?"

"I don't think you make that kind of mistake

shoving a needle in someone's arm. No, I think Keith was specifically targeted."

"But why? How would he get mixed up with criminals like this?"

"This is just a hunch, but I'm guessing he saw something he wasn't supposed to see."

"Like what?"

"I don't know," Hall replied. "A person's face, a transaction happening, somebody doing something to somebody else, something along those lines. I don't see what else it could be. He stumbled onto something."

Once at the pharmacy, they went inside, assuming they'd have to have the manager paged to the front of the store again. Luckily, this time Sharon was already up there, working on an end cap display.

"Hi, Sharon," Hall said pleasantly, knowing they weren't likely to be well-received.

She looked up at them, and they could already see the disgust on her face. She stood up, huffing at her attention being diverted from her work.

"Yes? What do you guys want now?"

"Just wanna talk for a minute."

"Why do you keep coming here? The last time you were here, there was a fight out in the parking lot. It seems like trouble follows you."

"Don't I know it."

"We just wanna ask you a few things, then we'll be out of your hair," Charlotte said.

"Yeah, until you come back again in a few more

days," Sharon replied. "Are you here to accuse me of something else? Because I really don't have time for that."

"No, we just want you to take a look at some pictures for us."

"Pictures?"

Hall took the pictures out of his pocket and handed them to her. "Can you identify any of these men?"

Sharon gave him an evil eye before taking the pictures, not really wanting to help them at all. She looked at each of the men carefully, even checking the pictures twice. She then pointed to Guzman.

"This guy. I've seen him before."

"You have?" Hall asked. "Where?"

"Here. A few times."

"You remember the last time? What were the circumstances?"

Sharon tried to remember. "I think it was about a week before Keith's death."

"Were they together?" Charlotte asked.

"Yeah. They were talking."

"You know what it was about?"

Sharon shook her head. "No, they were too far away. It wasn't inside the building."

"It was outside?" Hall asked.

"It was by Keith's car. He was done work. He clocked out, went outside, then I went outside a few seconds later to have a cigarette. That's when I saw them by Keith's car."

"Could you tell what it was about? Were they arguing?"

Sharon then pointed to Guzman's picture. "Well, this guy was doing most of the talking. It didn't look like arguing. Didn't look like Keith was saying much."

"What about the other guy? Did he seem heated?"

"It's tough to tell from so far away. It did look like a couple veins in his neck popped out a couple of times, so maybe he had something on his mind."

"And you saw him before that?" Charlotte asked.

"Yeah, I remember seeing him a few times in here."

"With Keith?"

Sharon tried to remember. "No, no, I don't think so. It was just... wait a minute. Yeah, there was another time I remember seeing them together. Maybe a month or so before I saw them at the car. I think this guy came in for a prescription or something, and then I saw them talking in the aisle for a minute, maybe not even that. They moved on really quickly. I just assumed the guy was asking Keith where a product was or something."

Hall and Charlotte looked at each other, feeling like they might have finally hit on something. Hall then got an idea that he was sure Sharon probably wasn't going to like.

"Would you happen to have an address for this guy?" Hall asked.

"Possibly."

"Is it possible we can see it?"

Sharon shook her head. "That's personal information. I can't share that with anyone unless there's a court order or warrant or something."

"I understand all that. But this guy's already dead."

Sharon looked a little in disbelief as she looked at the pair.

"That's right. He's dead. Keith's dead." Hall then pointed to Jernigan's picture. "See this guy here? You might be able to guess it, but yeah, he's dead too. In case you're not seeing the pattern, there's a lot of dead guys popping up lately. That's not a coincidence. Something's going on here. And we need to find out what it is before anyone else joins them."

"I still can't intentionally let you see someone's address in our files."

"How about... unintentionally?"

Sharon thought for a second, then sighed, not believing what she was about to do. "Follow me."

Hall and Charlotte gave each other a look, not sure what was going on, but they both followed the manager to the back of the store. They were led into the back office where Sharon sat down at a desk and started typing on a computer. She then picked up the phone on the desk and called the front cashier.

"Yeah, can you call me up to the front in about thirty seconds? Thanks."

None of the three said another word to each other as Sharon continued typing. She was seemingly finished and just sat there, staring at the screen. Then the call to the front came over the loudspeaker.

"Sharon to the front, Sharon to the front."

"I have to go," Sharon said. "I'll be back in a few minutes."

Hall looked at Charlotte and gave her a shrug, not sure what was happening as they watched the manager walk out of the office. Charlotte had an idea, though, and went over to the computer and sat down.

"What are you doing?" Hall asked.

Charlotte looked at him and smirked. "She was giving us access."

"Oh. She was doing the old, I'm not gonna let you see, but if you happen to glance at it when I'm not in the room, I can't be held liable trick."

"Uh, yeah, something like that."

"Find anything yet?"

Charlotte's fingers struck a few keys, though most of the work was already done for her. All she had to do was find Guzman's name. Once she did, she printed a copy. Hall went over to the printer and grabbed it.

"Hey, while we're here, why don't you check and see if any of our other friends are in there?"

"Sharon already said she didn't recognize them."

"Maybe she never saw them," Hall said. "Maybe they came in on her days off. Who knows?"

"Yeah, maybe."

Charlotte went back to work on the computer,

trying to pull up the names of Jernigan and Ellis, though neither were coming up in the files.

"Nothing."

"Well, it was worth a shot," Hall said.

Charlotte looked through the mirror that overlooked the store and saw Sharon making her way back. "All right, she's on her way, we gotta finish up."

Hall put the printout in his pocket as Charlotte put the computer screen back to the way Sharon had it. They quickly walked out of the office, meeting Sharon near the back of the store where the pain reliever aisle was.

"Did you guys find the bathroom OK?"

"Yes," Hall answered. "Yes, we did. Thank you."

Sharon nodded. "Hope it helps."

"So do we. Thank you again."

Hall and Charlotte walked out of the pharmacy and back to their car. Once inside, they sat there for a few minutes, beginning to read the printout they had taken from Sharon's office.

"Guess we were wrong about her," Charlotte said.

"Yeah, it would seem so."

"If she was mixed up in anything I doubt that she would have done that."

"Unless it doesn't lead to anything, and she knows it."

"Always cynical."

"That's the business we're in, isn't it? Believe no one

and keep asking questions until the puzzle fits together."

"Well, I'm thinking she's not involved now."

"I would tend to agree," Hall said. "Not a hundred percent, but I'm hovering in the nineties."

"Maybe she really did believe that Keith did it to himself."

"Seems that way."

Charlotte kept talking as Hall read the paper, but he wasn't hearing a word she was saying. After a minute of talking, she could tell that he was tuning her out.

"Are you listening to me?"

Hall put the paper in his lap as he stared out the front windshield. He was obviously deep in thought over something.

"Brandon?"

Hall looked down at the paper again, still not hearing a thing. Charlotte was starting to get annoyed at the lack of attention he was paying to her. She figured she would say something provocative. Maybe that would perk up his ears.

"Maybe I'll just take off all my clothes in the car right here."

Hall still wasn't paying attention.

"Maybe I should just run around in the streets naked."

Still nothing.

"Or maybe I should call that cute guy I know and

go out with him. He'd probably pay attention to me. Maybe have some drinks, get flirty, you know, all that stuff."

Hall finally looked at his girlfriend, though by the blank stare on his face, it was obvious he still didn't know what she'd said.

"Were you just saying something?"

Charlotte couldn't help but laugh to herself. "Oh, no, what gave you that idea?"

"Oh. I thought you said something."

"I did, but It's not important."

"What'd you say?"

"I was just asking if there was anything important in there. Looks like your mind is somewhere else."

"Oh, sorry, I was just thinking of something."

"No kidding?"

Hall then passed the paper over to her and pointed to Guzman's address. "Look at that address. Look familiar to you?"

"No. Why?"

"That's the point. It isn't familiar. That's not the same address we found his body at or the address of his apartment."

"So he used a fake address," Charlotte said. "I'm sure it's done sometimes. I doubt he's the first to do it."

"Probably not. But it does give us an additional lead to run down."

"Might not be anything. He might have just put any

address down, not even knowing or caring who lived there."

"Possible. And it's equally possible it could give us some additional answers or leads."

"Should we let Bradham know?"

"Not yet," Hall replied. "We'll run it down first and see what's shaking. If it's too deep, then we'll bring him in. First, we gotta see if there's anything to it."

21

As Hall and Charlotte drove to the new address they found associated with Jerry Guzman, Bradham called when they were about ten minutes away from it.

"Hey, how's it going?" Hall asked.

"Just peachy. I told you I'd call when we found out about Ellis' apartment."

"Anything?"

"Nah, it was empty."

"Kinda figured."

"Yeah, looked like he hadn't been there in a few days at least."

"Any leads inside?"

"Nothing worth mentioning."

"Does that mean there was something?"

"No," Bradham replied. "It means the only things

we found were small things that won't lead anywhere. It's a dead end."

"Oh."

"What are you up to now?"

"What do you mean?" Hall asked, trying to figure out if the detective already knew where he was going. He didn't know how Bradham would know, but he certainly implied that he knew something was up.

"I mean, what are you doing right now?"

"Nothing. Why?"

"Because I doubt you're just sitting at home on your hands. When I said we'd check out Ellis' place, you guys left rather easily, leading me to believe you had something else on your plate. Am I right?"

"No."

"I'm not?"

"No."

"So you got nothing else going on?"

"What else would we have going on?"

"I dunno. You tell me."

"Nothing right now," Hall said. "We just went back to the pizza shop, pharmacy, roommates, just to see if anyone recognized Guzman, Ellis, or Jernigan."

"Did they?"

"The manager at the pharmacy recognized Guzman there. Said she remembered him and Zeller having a few conversations."

"That would seem to indicate they knew each other more than everyone thought."

"Yeah, seems to."

"So what else you got on your plate?"

"Nothing."

"C'mon, Brandon, do you really expect me to believe you've got nothing else?"

"Why would I have anything else?"

"Because you've been two steps ahead of us on this whole thing the entire time," Bradham said. "I don't expect that to change now."

"So you don't believe it's an overdose anymore either?"

"No, and neither does anybody else. So stop playing games and just tell me what you know."

"I don't know anything."

"Hold your phone up in the air."

"What?" Hall asked, thinking it was a strange request.

"Hold your phone up and stop talking. I wanna hear what's going on around you."

"Why?"

"Because I want to see if you're actually at home or if I can hear noises that would tell me you're somewhere else."

"That's a little intrusive, don't you think?"

"Brandon, I wanna know exactly what you're doing right now. If I have to, I can run you in for operating without a license."

"You can't do that?"

"You wanna make a bet? Just tell me what you're

doing so I can help."

Hall sighed, knowing he was going to have to open up. He didn't think Bradham would really run him in. That was just the tough-talking cop in him coming out. But still, it was enough of a threat to spur Hall into coming clean.

"All right, fine. We came across another address that's associated with Guzman. We're going to check it out now."

"What address? How'd you get it?"

"It was an address he gave at the pharmacy while picking up a prescription."

"What prescription?" Bradham asked.

"OxyContin."

"OxyContin? What doctor prescribed it?"

Hall had to look down at the paper again to find the name. "Doctor Martin McCord."

"Martin McCord. That name sounds familiar for some reason. Is that McCord's address that you're going to?"

"I dunno. I guess we'll find out when we get there."

"It's probably not. I've heard of this guy before, and I can't remember where."

"Maybe someone else you busted used him as a doctor."

"No, that's not it," Bradham said. "Listen, I'm gonna do some digging on this McCord. I'm almost sure I know him from somewhere. When you get to that address you're going to, just sit on it for a while, OK?"

"What?"

"Just stake it out for a while. Don't move on it."

"Why?"

"Will you just listen to me? Don't do anything except watch. And when we get off the phone, text me the address."

"Why?"

"So I can be there."

"OK."

"I'll call you again in a little bit."

After getting off the phone, Charlotte asked about the conversation. As Hall started to explain, he texted the address to Bradham.

"What was that about?"

"I dunno. Bradham says he thinks he knows the doctor who prescribed the medication for Guzman. He wants us to just sit on this apartment and not go in or anything."

"Sounds like good advice."

"Yeah, we'll see."

"We'll see about whether it's good advice or we'll see about going in?"

Hall gave her a devilish kind of smile. "Both."

"Oh, Brandon, you're not gonna listen, are you?"

"I don't know. We'll see."

Once they got to the apartment in question, they were hardly surprised by what they saw. Another building that wasn't exactly on the upper end of the scale.

"You think just once we could find someplace that doesn't look like the roof's caving in?" Charlotte asked. "Maybe a doorman, an indoor pool, balconies, flowers in front, things like that?"

"Doormen went out of style in the forties."

"You know what I mean. Just once I'd like to go into one of these places and not have to worry about stepping on mice and rats."

The building wasn't exactly like the others. It was an apartment, but it was a condo unit, not an entire apartment building. Several condos in the area were used as rentals. The one Hall and Charlotte were looking at was an end unit that had seen better days. It wasn't falling apart or anything, but needed some fresh paint on the outside, and the roof was about thirty years old, so it was in need of some upkeep. They waited a few minutes before something occurred to Charlotte.

"What are we sitting here for?"

"What do you mean?" Hall asked.

"Who are we waiting for?"

"I dunno… anybody."

"The address is associated with Guzman, right? Well, he's dead. So is Jernigan. Are we just expecting Ellis or Rankin to swing by for some reason?"

Hall stared blankly at the condo. Charlotte had a point. But it was also possible that maybe he shared the condo with others.

"How do we know he was the only one living

here?" Hall asked. "Maybe he had roommates here too."

"He had two apartments? Why? The one he was found dead in had clothes, food in the kitchen; he was definitely living there. He worked in a pizza shop. I doubt he brought in enough money to afford two places. And if he did, why wouldn't he just combine his money to get a better place instead of splitting it between these two places?"

"Well, if he was living at the other place, then what's he doing here? And why even put this address down at all? Why not use the other one?"

"A lot of questions that don't make any sense."

"The questions make a lot of sense," Hall said. "It's the answers that are confusing."

"How long are we going to sit here?"

Hall looked at the time. "I don't know. Let's give it another hour and see if anything pops out."

They waited outside the condo for another hour, not seeing anyone come even close to the address. They kept their eyes peeled for any activity inside the house as well, like curtains moving, shadows in a window, lights turning on or off, but there was nothing. There were plenty of empty parking spaces, and units were not given assigned spaces, so it was tough to know if there was a car there that belonged to the unit in question.

"I don't think anyone's here," Charlotte said.

"Yeah, I'm thinking you're right."

"We gonna sit here all night?"

"Nope."

"Then what?"

"We're gonna see if anyone's there," Hall answered.

"How are we gonna do that?"

Hall looked at her and smiled. "We're gonna knock."

"No. Brandon, I don't think that's a good idea."

"Why not?"

"Because what if someone dangerous is inside?"

Hall shrugged. "Then they'll meet someone dangerous outside."

"Brandon, this is not a good idea."

"Relax. It's either sit here and wait or start shaking some trees and see what falls out."

"Yeah, what if a coconut shakes out and hits you on the head and knocks you out?"

Hall opened his door. "You wait here."

"Why?"

"In case someone is there and something happens, you can call for backup."

"Gee, thanks. You know I don't like being far away from you in times like this."

"You'll be fine."

"What about you?"

"Well, if I get into trouble, call for help, then come running."

"We really need to work on your plans," Charlotte said.

"It'll be fine."

Hall closed the door, then slowly walked over to the end-unit condo. He still kept his eyes peeled on the windows, looking for movement, though he still didn't see any. He walked up to the door and loudly knocked three times. He took a step back and looked at the windows out of the corner of his eye. He was trying not to turn his head and make it look obvious that he was looking for someone. He was trying to be as nonchalant as possible. After a minute with no response, Hall moved closer to the door again, knocking five more times. This time, he stayed right on the door, putting his ear to it to see if he could hear any movement inside. There was still nothing though.

Hall turned around to look at Charlotte and threw his hands up to signal that he didn't have anything. Charlotte mumbled under her breath, hoping that her boyfriend would just walk back to the car. Knowing him like she did, she had a feeling it wouldn't be so simple. It turned out she was right. Instead of coming back to the car, Hall started walking around the side of the condo.

"What are you doing?" Charlotte whispered.

Hall continued walking around the condo until he reached the back, out of sight from Charlotte. She gave him a minute to come back around, but he never did. She huffed and puffed, then stormed out of the car, not liking Hall being out of her line of sight. Hall was pulling on the back-door handle, hoping it was open.

No such luck though. It was a regular door, with six small panes of glass that went from the midpoint of the door up to the top. Hall stood there looking at it, wishing there was a way he could get inside. He looked down, not really sure what he was looking for. He turned around, then saw a good-sized rock lying there by the house. He picked it up, then smashed a piece of the glass with the rock, shattering the single pane. Hall dropped the rock, then reached inside the new hole in the door, blindly finding the lock and unlocking it.

Before Hall had a chance to open the door, he heard someone coming. He heard the crunching sound of someone stepping on leaves, and it sounded pretty close. He went over to the corner of the house, waiting for whoever was coming. He cocked his arm back, ready to unload on whatever face turned the corner. Five seconds later, Charlotte came into his sight. Hall quickly pulled his arm back down as Charlotte jumped back, startled from the encounter.

"What are you doing?" Hall asked.

"What are you doing?"

"I asked first."

"You said you were going to knock on the door. What are you doing back here?"

"Just wanted to see what was back here."

"Now you see," Charlotte said. "Can we go now?"

"We can't."

"Why not?"

Hall then pointed to the door. "Look, the door's open. We can check inside."

Charlotte squinted her eyes as she looked at the door, not believing it had been like that. "Brandon, we can't just break into someone's house."

"We're not. It was already open." He then pointed to the glass. "Look, looks like someone already broke in before."

"Brandon, you just did that right now."

"I did not."

"What was that glass I heard breaking as I was coming back here?"

Hall shrugged. "I dunno. Must've stepped on some."

As Charlotte shook her head in disapproval, her eyes happened to glance down at the ground. She saw the large rock only a few inches away from the door where Hall dropped it. She reached down and picked it up, noticing a few glass fragments still stuck to it.

"What do you call this?"

"Looks like a rock," Hall said.

Charlotte gritted her teeth. "I know it's a rock. What do you call these sharp little shiny pieces on it?"

"Looks like pieces of glass."

"Do I look like I'm dumb?"

"You certainly do not."

"Then why can't you just tell me what happened?"

"Well, I guess whoever broke into this place the last

time probably used that rock in your hand. That's why there's still glass on it."

Charlotte tossed the rock back down to the ground, then put her hands on her hips. "Really? You're gonna lie to me like that?"

"If you don't know the truth, then you don't have to lie if you're ever asked about it."

"That's not a good strategy."

"Only one I got right now."

Charlotte shook her head and sighed. "Let's go."

"Go where?"

"Back to the car."

"No, I'm going in here," Hall said, pointing to the condo.

"You can't be serious."

"Charlotte, nobody's here right now and the door's open. Now if we stand here all day arguing about it, that might change soon. So let's hurry up and do this so we can get out of here."

Charlotte's shoulders slumped, knowing she was fighting a losing battle. "I don't like this."

"You don't have to like it. We just have to do it."

"*We* do not have to do anything."

"Well, you can stand here or go back to the car if you want to. I'm going in."

"This is not a good idea."

22

Hall and Charlotte went into the house and started searching around, hoping something of interest would jump out at them, bodies excluded, of course. They went into the kitchen and Hall opened the refrigerator.

"This is not the time to get something to eat," Charlotte joked.

"Just wanna see if someone's living here. If there's food in the fridge, good chance someone is."

"Well?"

"Box of pizza," Hall said, opening the box. There was one slice left.

After searching through the kitchen, they went into the living room, finding the room mostly filled with dust.

"This place needs a good cleaning," Charlotte said.

"Don't think it's high on their priority list."

There were a few papers on an end table that had a lamp sitting on it. Hall went over and looked through them. It was nothing that would provide any leads though. They spent another ten minutes going through the downstairs before making their way up to the second floor. In order to save some time, Hall and Charlotte searched in different rooms. There were three bedrooms and a bathroom on the floor. They went through two of the bedrooms, not finding a thing. Then Charlotte took the bathroom as Hall took the last bedroom.

"How come I always seem to get the bathroom?"

"I dunno," Hall said. "I figure you spend so much time in it yourself that you're more comfortable in it than I am." He couldn't even keep a straight face as he said it, not able to control his laughter.

"Oh, really? I take a long time in the bathroom? That's what you're saying?"

"Well… if the shoe fits."

"I'm gonna take that shoe and whack you over the head with it."

Charlotte finished up the bathroom and joined her boyfriend searching through the last bedroom.

"Doesn't look to me like anyone's lived here," Charlotte said. "I mean, look at the beds. They're all made, and it doesn't look like they've been slept in. There's hardly anything anywhere else either."

"Yeah, they probably just used this place as a spot for meetings, things like that."

Hall had just finished looking under the bed, then went to the closet as it was the last place to check. He opened the doors, not expecting to see anything. There was a black backpack sitting on the floor though. He looked back at Charlotte, who saw it too. Hall picked it up and brought it over to the bed. He unzipped it, then leaned forward as he looked inside. There were several packages that were wrapped in some kind of brown paper. Hall took them out and placed them on the bed where he carefully unwrapped them. Once the packages were opened, they observed a white powdery substance stuffed inside a bunch of smaller plastic bags.

"Is that what I think it is?" Charlotte asked.

"Well, I doubt it's sugar."

Hall reached back down into the bag again and felt a few more plastic bags. He brought them out, but this time he wasn't grabbing heroin bags. They were needles wrapped in plastic, almost like they just came from a factory, never before been used. Hall put them on the bed next to the other bags, then dug his hand into the backpack again. He found a few slips of paper and started reading them. He immediately knew they'd hit pay dirt.

"This is the stuff you need to use on Zeller," the note read. *"Make sure you use a clean needle, then inject so*

much into him there's no doubt it's an overdose. It needs to be done soon. They're getting worried about him. RJ."

Hall read the note three times, each time not really believing what he was seeing.

"What's the matter?" Charlotte asked. "You can't keep your eyes off that paper."

Hall just looked at her without saying anything. He still had that same worried look in his eye though. He went back to reading the paper again, sure he was seeing things or making it up in his own mind. But he wasn't. It was right there in black and white and messy handwriting. He looked at Charlotte again, who was still concerned about what was going on.

"Brandon, what's wrong?"

Hall still didn't reply. Instead, he just reached his hand out, the paper still between his fingers. Charlotte wrestled the sheet out of his hand and began reading it. She was as dumbfounded at the content of the note as her boyfriend was.

"This can't be for real," Charlotte said.

"RJ. Robbie Jernigan."

Charlotte read it a couple more times as well, then lowered it back down. "So this is it. This is the evidence we needed. This proves that Jernigan and Guzman were in on it."

"Yeah."

Charlotte looked at him curiously. Though he agreed, Hall certainly didn't seem happy or excited about their findings. She thought he would have been pleased. Instead, he looked far from it. He actually seemed somewhat disappointed for some reason.

"What's the matter? Aren't you happy we found this? This proves that Keith didn't kill himself."

Hall continued looking in the backpack. "Yeah. Yeah, I am."

Though he said he was, Charlotte could tell that wasn't true. There was no excitement in his voice, and his facial expression indicated he wasn't that thrilled. She could tell.

"What's the matter?"

"Nothing," Hall replied.

"Don't nothing me. I can tell by now when something's bothering you. What is it?"

Hall finished looking in the bag, not finding anything else of significance. "You really wanna know?"

"That's why I asked."

"This is all too... neat."

Charlotte scrunched her face together, not sure what he was talking about. "What do you mean, neat?"

"It's just all too coincidental. We just happen to find a backpack with a bunch of heroin and a note in it? I mean, seriously, who leaves a note like that laying around for someone to find it?"

"Well, they probably didn't think someone was going to break into the house and start snooping around."

Hall shook his head, still not buying it. "C'mon,

Charlotte, who leaves a note like that implicating themselves in a crime? What would be the point? It only takes two seconds to rip it up and throw it out."

"Maybe Guzman was hanging on to it in case he got arrested? That way he had something hanging over Jernigan to make sure nothing ever happened to him. In fact, maybe that's why Jernigan killed him. Because he knew Guzman had evidence implicating him too, so Jernigan had to stop him."

Maybe that made sense in some way, but not to Hall. He wasn't buying it. It was all too convenient.

"Why are you finding that so hard to believe?" Charlotte asked.

"Because I'm not a big believer in happenstance. We just happen to walk in and find this stuff. Big coincidence."

"It does happen, you know."

"Maybe."

"So... so what exactly are you saying?"

"Maybe this was planted here hoping we would find it," Hall said.

"Why? For what purpose? These guys are dead. They can't plant anything."

"Exactly," Hall said. "These guys are dead. They can't refute anything. Just think for a minute. If someone else was involved in this, and they were really the ones behind everything, what better way to get out from under it? You've got two dead guys, you put a backpack of heroin, needles, and a note from one of the dead men, and everything comes down on them. The case gets wrapped up, the dead men are charged with the crime, and they're not alive to say anything to the contrary. All pretty neat, huh?"

Charlotte ran her hands through her hair, thinking of everything Hall just said. "I dunno. Maybe. But maybe not. Maybe you're thinking this through too much."

"Maybe. We need to call Bradham and get his team out here to process everything."

They went outside and called Detective Bradham and told him what they'd found. Bradham called it in and had a nearby patrol car get to the house first. Once the patrol car got there, Hall and Charlotte informed them of what was going on. They stayed nearby as they waited for Bradham to get on scene. As they waited, they continued their discussion about what they thought was going on.

"Doesn't this strike you as funny?" Hall asked.

"What?"

"Sharon."

"Are we back to her again?"

"No, just listen to me."

"OK."

"She's argumentative this entire time. Every time we've talked to her she's tried to steer us in a different direction, right?"

"Right," Charlotte replied.

"So what happens this last time? She's completely helpful. Like out of the blue she's a different person. Kind, helpful, believing everything we say, like she's a changed person."

"People are allowed to change their minds, you know."

Hall pretty much ignored that statement. "And the one time she is helpful, look what happens? We just happen to come here and find this stuff, all neat and cozy. She didn't give us much of an argument about looking at that address if you remember."

"I remember." Charlotte laughed. "So what are you saying? That Sharon's behind all of this? That she deliberately wanted us to come to this address so we could find this stuff?"

"Think about it. If she's involved, and this winds up being the end of it, she gets to walk away no questions asked. No more pesky investigators, no more questions, no more anything. She's in the clear."

"Brandon, I think you're way overthinking all of this."

"Yeah, maybe, but you can't deny that it might be a possibility."

Charlotte sighed. "OK, maybe it's a possibility. A slight one. But I think you're way off base with this."

"Maybe. We'll run it by Bradham when he gets here."

"He's not gonna be that happy you went in there, you know."

Hall took a gulp, not really wanting to listen to the detective lecture him when he arrived. He knew Charlotte was probably right that he most likely would.

"It'll be fine," Hall said, hoping more than knowing. "Everything's fine. I hope."

23

By the time Bradham and the rest of the crime scene investigation unit arrived, Hall and Charlotte had moved around to the back of the building. Judging by the scowl on the detective's face, Hall assumed he wasn't that glad to be there.

"What do you think you're doing?"

"What do you mean?" Hall asked.

"What are you doing?"

"I don't know what you're talking about."

"You deliberately disobeyed and disregarded what I told you to do."

"I did not."

"I told you to sit on the house and watch it, didn't I? I told you not to go in and just stake it out for a bit, didn't I? Didn't I say that?"

"I don't remember if you did or not."

"I almost certainly did," Bradham said.

Hall tried to remember their conversation, but honestly couldn't remember much of it. Bradham could have said it and Hall just ignored that part.

"Why are you so angry?"

"Because I told you not to move on this place, and you went ahead and did it anyway."

"I don't even remember you saying that," Hall said.

"Well, I did." Bradham then looked at Charlotte. "Didn't you hear me tell him that?"

"Uh, I couldn't hear," Charlotte replied. "He didn't have the phone on speaker."

"Well, I did." Bradham looked back at Hall again. "You know, Brandon, you're starting to turn into a little bit of a maverick."

"No, I'm not."

"Yes, you are. You go off and do what you want no matter what you're told."

Hall shrugged. "I'm just going where the evidence takes me."

"If you don't start watching it and being more careful, it's going to take you right to a ten by ten cell."

"Well, I'm sorry, Dad, I didn't mean to upset you so much."

"Don't give me that. I just want you to start doing things a little more by the book."

"I'm not a by-the-book guy, Steven. I'm not a cop."

"Yeah, and you're not even technically a private

investigator either," Bradham said. "Right now, you're just a private citizen who's becoming a big pain in my ass."

"Listen, Buster, I don't have to take any of that from you..."

"Who are you calling Buster?"

They started arguing a little more, and it was getting a little too heated for Charlotte's tastes. The two men moved in closer to each other, making her worried they were about to come to blows, though it might have just been her fearing the worst. She quickly moved in between them, putting one of her hands on each of the front of their shoulders to back them up a little and create some distance between them.

"Boys, boys...," Charlotte said. "Let's calm it down. We're all friends here, no need to get overly emotional and say things we don't mean."

Bradham adjusted his tie and suit jacket. "I'm fine. I'm not emotional."

"I'm not either," Hall said.

Charlotte looked up at the sky and rolled her eyes, not believing she actually had to do this. She thought this type of behavior stopped in the ninth grade. She looked at each of the men and started lecturing them.

"If you two are done yapping at each other like a bunch of four-year-olds, let's not forget why we're here, huh? There is a reason we're all here right now, right?"

Bradham, still a little hot under the collar, looked

at her and nodded, though he still had an unpleasant expression on his face. "Yeah."

Charlotte then looked at Hall. "Right?"

Hall shrugged. "I guess."

"So are you two done? Can we get on with why we're here?"

Both men nodded, though neither looked at her. They were a little embarrassed they had to be scolded like they were elementary school children.

"OK, Charlotte's right," Bradham said. "Let's just put all that aside and focus on this. Go back to the beginning."

Hall then explained how they wound up at that address, then how they wound up finding the backpack.

"Wait a minute," Bradham said. "Are you telling me you broke in here?"

"No, I'm not telling you that. When I got here, the door was already open. I wouldn't just break into a house for no reason."

Charlotte turned her head, put her hand over her mouth and cleared her throat, knowing full well that was a lie.

"Is that how it happened Charlotte?" Bradham asked.

"Uh, yeah, well, yeah, the door was definitely already open when I saw it."

Bradham's eyes quickly fluttered between the pair,

not sure he believed it. In fact, he was pretty positive they were lying. At least one of them was.

"You both got back here at the same time?"

They both answered at the same time. "Yes," Hall said. "No," Charlotte said.

Bradham's shoulders dropped. "You two can't even get your story straight? So you didn't get back here at the same time?"

Hall and Charlotte looked at each other and answered simultaneously again. "No," Hall said. "Yes," Charlotte replied. They both looked at each other again, wondering why the other one changed their answer.

Bradham put his hands up, not wanting to deal with it anymore. "You know what, forget it. You both got here at the same time and the door was open. OK?" He then started mumbling under his breath and reached into his jacket pocket. He removed some aspirin and threw a couple pills in his mouth and swallowed. "Really can't deal with this stuff anymore. Driving me crazy."

"That's pretty impressive," Hall said. "Taking aspirin without something to wash it down."

"I've had a lot of practice lately."

"I bet. You seem tense."

Bradham glared at him, looking like he was about to go off on him again. Luckily, he was able to control it and keep himself calm. "I am fine."

"Good."

"OK, let's stop the chatting out here and go take a look inside."

Hall and Charlotte followed the detective inside, directing him to where the backpack was found. Hall left it on the bed.

"Don't touch anything else," Bradham said. "I'll have the place dusted for prints."

Bradham put on gloves, then started going through the backpack, examining its contents as Hall and Charlotte stood in the background. After Bradham was done, he took his friends back out of the house.

"We're gonna need you guys to head down to the station and get your fingerprints."

"Why?" Charlotte asked.

"Because if your fingerprints are on anything, we wanna be able to compare them to any other prints we find in there. So if we find yours or anything, we can just eliminate them. You guys already contaminated the scene enough."

"What do you mean contaminated?" Hall asked.

"You touched almost everything in there."

"Well, how else are you going to find out what's inside something unless you open it?"

"As soon as you found something you should've called it in."

"And what if there wasn't anything in it? Then I would've had to listen to you complaining about being called down here for no reason."

"Back to that again? That's why I told you to sit tight on everything. I told you I was going to come."

"No, you didn't."

"Yes, I did," Bradham said. "Charlotte, you better get his ears checked, because he's not listening too well."

"Get your own ears checked, pal."

Charlotte didn't want to listen to any more of their feuding and stepped between them again.

"Boys, boys, let's calm it down. Remember, we're all friends here. We're all after the same thing."

"OK, OK," Bradham said.

"So do you need anything else from us?"

"No, just head to the station so we can get your prints."

"What about the Zeller case?" Hall asked.

"What about it?"

"You gonna reclassify it now to a murder?"

"Not yet."

"Why not?"

"No proof yet."

"No proof? What do you call that note in there?"

"I call it a good lead," Bradham replied.

"A good lead? What the hell is wrong with you?"

"Listen, Brandon, we work things differently in the police department that you might not be aware of. We can't just go off half-cocked making assumptions. It looks like it might be heroin up there, but it needs to be tested. It looks like Jernigan wrote a letter up there, but it needs to be analyzed. It looks like there might be fingerprints in the house, but it needs to be checked. These are the things we're required to do in the police department. Double and triple check to make sure our facts are straight so we don't accuse innocent people of a crime."

"What innocent people are we accusing? Everyone in this case is winding up dead."

"Be that as it may, we still have to do our job. By the book."

"Oh, for crying out loud. And how long is all that gonna take?"

"Could be days, could be weeks, could be months. All depends on how busy the lab is."

"Months?" Hall asked. "Are you serious? Months? Just to have someone look at a piece of paper and see if the handwriting matches up? Are you kidding?"

"No, I'm not kidding. The lab might have hundreds of things going on right now. They work on whatever's the highest priority thing they have at that moment."

"What could be a higher priority than this? We're talking about a murder."

"I understand that."

"No, we're actually talking about two murders... no, three, three bodies. Three murders. Zeller, Guzman, and Jernigan. And it might be four if we ever find out where Ellis is. He might be lying face first in a pool right now for all we know," Hall said.

"Do you think I don't know that? If you would ever

let me finish a sentence, I might tell you what my plans are."

"Well, what are they?"

"I was going to tell you I was going to ask the lab to put a rush on it so we can hopefully have it back within a week."

"Oh," Hall said, almost looking embarrassed that he was giving the detective a hard time. "Sorry."

"What about that doctor you were telling Brandon about?" Charlotte asked. "How's he fit in with all of this?"

"Yeah, what was his name? McCord or something?"

"Martin McCord," Bradham said.

"What's his story?"

"He's a doctor who's been under investigation for selling and writing illegal prescriptions."

"He's not in jail?"

"Not yet. I'm not the investigating officer, so I didn't have a chance to look at the full details, but from what I understand, they don't have enough evidence yet to make a conviction."

"Well, maybe that's our next move," Hall said. "Why don't we all go over to his office and see if he can tell us something about Guzman? I mean, he obviously knows him if he wrote the prescription."

"Can't."

"Why not?"

"Because McCord's not in his office."

"OK, so we'll go to his house."

"Not that easy."

"Why not?"

"Because he's not there either," Bradham answered.

"Well then, where is he?"

"Don't know. He's flown the coop."

Hall scrunched his eyebrows together, like he was having difficulty understanding what was being said, though it was more just him being shocked. "What do you mean he's flown the coop?"

"I mean he's gone bye-bye. That's why it took so long for me to get over here. I went to McCord's office to talk to him, and he wasn't there. Place wasn't even open. Then we checked his home address and there was nobody there either."

"Maybe he's just taking the day off."

"I think it's more likely he knows he's in deep shit and is trying to get out of here."

"How would he know we're on to him?" Hall asked.

"Like I said, this guy's been on the radar for a while. It's not like he just popped up today. Could be he got wind of something. Who knows? If we knew how some of these people got their information, we'd have a lot more of them locked up."

"What about that Rankin guy, how does he fit into all of this?"

"We don't know if he does. Just because Jernigan was at his place doesn't mean Rankin was involved."

Hall rubbed the top of his head and sighed. "I hate this whole thing."

"Welcome to my world. Let's head down to the station so we can get your prints."

"What about Ellis?"

"We've got some feelers out on him," Bradham answered. "We're working some informants to see if they've heard anything. Hopefully one of them will turn something."

Hall and Charlotte went back to their car so they could go down to the police station. As they drove, they talked about the case.

"Looks like this is basically wrapped up," Charlotte said.

"I'm not so sure."

"Why? If that turns out to be Jernigan's handwriting, that basically proves they gave something to Keith."

"I just don't know how all this fits together. We still don't even know why Zeller was killed. What did he get himself into? How does a regular college kid get mixed up with the likes of this bunch?"

"Maybe it has something to do with the prescriptions. Think about it. If this Dr. McCord was handing out phony prescriptions, and we know Guzman was in on it, and Keith worked at a pharmacy, maybe he somehow discovered it? Maybe he saw something, overheard something, and that's why they went after him," Charlotte said.

"Well, I guess that could be. McCord and Ellis might be our last chance to figure out what went on here. If they're in the wind, we might never find out what really happened."

"How are we gonna find these guys? I mean, we don't even have a starting place with them."

"Well, I think we might just have to get lucky."

24

Five days had passed since finding the backpack. Though Hall and Charlotte had debated telling Olivia Zeller about her brother, they decided to wait until they got the official report back about the handwriting. They didn't want to tell her one thing and get her hopes up, only to then have to go back and say something else and dash them if the results weren't what they assumed they would be.

In the meantime, they started investigating both McCord and Ellis, trying to find at least one, if not both of them. Hall and Charlotte checked out all of the known addresses that were associated with them: businesses, offices, homes, places they were known to hang out, but it all led nowhere. They seemed to have disappeared.

Hall and Charlotte were sitting at the kitchen table in her apartment, going over a bunch of files and papers, still trying to do what they could to find their targets.

"Maybe we should take another run at Sharon," Charlotte said.

Hall was surprised. "You wanna take another run at Sharon? What for?"

"I get the feeling she knows something."

"Well, I've been telling you that from the beginning."

"Yeah, but now I feel it too."

"What brought this on?"

"It all seems to fit together. If McCord was doing these illegal prescriptions, since Sharon was the manager, don't you think she would've seen something funny going on?"

"Yeah, I do."

"And it's like you said, she wasn't very helpful, then all of a sudden she gets a heart and gives us an address where we just happen to find something that ties off Keith's death?"

"I know," Hall said. "Very suspect."

"Let's go take another run at her."

"I dunno."

"What? Now you're the one holding back on her?"

"Well, Steven called me yesterday and told me to stay away from her because they were planning on serving a warrant or something and looking at their files or something like that. I was only paying half attention."

"Since when did you ever listen to that?"

Hall raised an eyebrow. "Valid point."

"I'll call the store to see if she's there today."

"OK."

Charlotte called the pharmacy to see if Sharon was working. They didn't want to just show up only to find out it was her off day. Hall continued looking through their files as his girlfriend called. He wasn't paying much attention to what she was doing. After a minute, Charlotte sat back down at the table.

"She's not there," Charlotte said. "She's off today."

"Oh."

"Let's swing by her house and have a chat."

Hall leaned back, wondering if this was the same woman he was used to. "You're getting all gung-ho all of a sudden."

"I feel we're close and can wrap it up soon. What? Are you getting afraid of her or something?"

"Really?"

"Then c'mon, let's go. Maybe if we're lucky, we'll find her going out and tail her somewhere. Maybe she's in cahoots with the others and will lead us to them," Charlotte said.

"That's a lot of maybes right there."

"Well, maybe it's true. Are you gonna come? Or are you gonna make me go alone?"

"Just keep your pants on, of course I'll go with you."

They left the apartment and hopped in their car, though this time Hall did the driving. It was a fifteen-minute drive to Sharon's home. She lived in a colonial in a nice neighborhood. A much different atmosphere than they'd been used to. A welcomed change from Charlotte's perspective. As they pulled up to the house, Charlotte pointed to the driveway.

"Her car's still here."

Hall parked along the curb. "Well, let's go take a look."

They got out of the car and took a quick look around, as was becoming customary for them, to make sure trouble wasn't shooting towards them. It seemed to be a quiet neighborhood, as only the sound of the breeze and some birds chirping could be heard.

"Seems like a nice area," Charlotte said.

"Yeah."

They approached the house, almost expecting the door to suddenly swing open with Sharon appearing in the frame of it. It didn't happen though. They went up to the door and knocked a few times. There was no answer. They knocked a few more times. Still nothing.

"You stay here," Hall said. "I'm gonna check around back."

"Brandon..."

Hall put his hands up to calm her down, already knowing what she was thinking. "Just relax, I'm not gonna do anything. I'm just gonna check, OK?"

Hall went around the side of the house, checking in every window he came across. All the curtains were closed. He eventually hopped a small chain-link fence, only about four feet high, and moved around to the back of the house. There was a small enclosed patio off the back, and Hall went over to it, pulled on the door and opened it. He cautiously went inside, not giving a second thought about it. Everything looked neat and clean. He walked over to the door that led to the house, not expecting it to be open... but it was. He briefly thought of Charlotte, but it wasn't like he actually broke in this time. This time it really was open. Though if Sharon really was in there, she was not going to be happy about seeing him in her house. That's why he'd have to be careful and try not to be seen. Of course, if Sharon kept checking the front, where Charlotte was, she might not have noticed Hall coming in through the back.

The door that Hall went in actually led to the garage, which also had a door leading into the house. Hall turned the handle to the door, slowly opening it. He peeked his head in, hoping he didn't get whacked with anything. He opened the door further, enough for his body to slink its way through. He stood in the dining room, ready to look around, though he wouldn't have to for long. Right off the dining room was an open kitchen, and Hall immediately saw it. Sharon's body lying on the floor. Hall moved around the dining room table to check on her condition, but it didn't take much to see that she was dead. There was blood splatter on the walls, a pool of blood around her body, especially her head where the bullet went through, and there was a gun next to her.

Hall's shoulders slumped, not expecting this type of scene at all. Before doing anything else, he took a quick look around the kitchen, searching for anything obvious that stood out. Basically, any type of lead that might have been lying around on a counter or on a table somewhere, something that might lead them to Ellis or McCord. Unfortunately, there was nothing to be found. It was a remarkably clean kitchen area, outside of all the blood. Dejectedly, he went over to the front door and opened it. Charlotte was quite surprised to see his face.

"What are you doing in there?"

"Sharon's dead," Hall said with disappointment.

"What?"

"Found her lying on the kitchen floor with a bullet in her head."

Charlotte put her hand on her face. "Oh, no."

"Guess we better call Steve and let him know."

"How'd you get in there?" Charlotte asked, concerned that he broke in again.

"Just went around the back and found the doors unlocked."

Charlotte gave him a look that indicated she didn't believe him. "Really?"

"No, they really were unlocked this time. I'm not fooling about that."

Charlotte took a step inside, but Hall blocked her from going any further. "Where is she?"

"You don't wanna see that. It's not a pretty sight."

"I've seen dead bodies before."

"Yeah, but it's not something you wanna get used to either. Let's just wait outside until the cops show up."

They went back to their car and called Bradham and told him what they'd found. Within a few minutes a police car showed up. Hall and Charlotte talked to them about their discovery, and the police started taping off the scene. A few more police cars rolled up right after that. About twenty minutes later, Bradham showed up. Seeing Hall and Charlotte standing by their car, he walked right over to them.

"Can you tell me why you seem to be the point person at every crime scene we have now?"

Hall smiled. "Just lucky, I guess."

"So what happened?" Hall then retold everything they did. "You touch anything?"

"Just the handles on the patio door, the door that led into the garage, the door that led into the house, and the inside part of the front door."

"Funny how you're able to always get inside these places."

"Is it my fault people don't lock their doors anymore?"

"Didn't touch anything inside? The body, a chair, counter, anything like that?"

Hall shook his head. "Nope. Saw the body, opened

the front door and told Charlotte. Came back here to the car and called you."

"What were you guys doing here?"

Hall crossed his arms and shrugged. "I dunno. We got the idea that she knew more than what she had told us. Thought it was convenient that the one time she was helpful to us, it led to a discovery that could close the case."

"So you thought she was in on it and deliberately led you there to turn down the heat?"

"That's the thought."

"What are you thinking now?"

"Beats the hell out of me," Hall replied. "I've got so many thoughts on this case my head's about to burst."

Charlotte wanted to make sure they weren't going to jump to the obvious conclusion. "You guys aren't really thinking she committed suicide, are you?"

"What else would it be?" Bradham asked.

"Look, everyone else in this case has been murdered, right? Keith, Guzman, Jernigan, now Sharon."

"Well, it's too soon to jump to that conclusion either way. Which reminds me, I should be in there investigating instead of standing out here jabbering with you two."

"You need us to stick around here for anything?" Hall asked. "We already gave our statements to one of the other guys."

"Yeah, go ahead. Where are you gonna be?"

"Why?"

"Just wanna know where and when I should dispatch the next units to."

Hall smiled. "That's funny. Really amusing."

"I thought so. But seriously, where are you going from here?"

Hall looked at Charlotte and threw his hands up. "I dunno. Nowhere specific. Guess we'll figure that part out."

"Oh, you mean you don't have another lead already that you haven't told me about. Seems to be the way things have been going lately."

"Well, you know how it is. I'm sure something will turn up."

25

Hall and Charlotte drove around for a while, trying to figure out their next move. Eventually, after not knowing what else to do, they went back to their apartment. Only thirty minutes after getting back, Hall's phone rang. It was an unfamiliar number.

"Hello?"

"Hey, you're Brandon Hall, the PI?"

"No, well, yeah, maybe, depends on who you are."

"My name's Ellis. I understand you're looking for me."

Hall's eyes almost bulged out of his head. It was a call he never expected. "How'd you get my number?"

"Does that really matter now? You wanna talk or not?"

"Yeah, sure. What's on your mind?"

"I wanna talk to you."

"So go ahead and talk," Hall said.

"Not over the phone. Wanna meet in person."

"Why?"

"Because I need to try to get out from under this thing. It's all gone sideways."

"In what way?"

"Listen, Guzman killed that college kid, all right? Then Jernigan killed Guzman because he was afraid he was gonna talk."

"So who killed Jernigan?"

"I don't know. Must've been something else he was working on."

"Maybe it was James Rankin, huh?"

"Rankin? Who the hell is that?"

"Isn't he the guy behind all of this?" Hall asked.

"I don't know who this Rankin guy is. Never heard of him."

"So what do you want with me?"

"I can give you some evidence that ties all this together. Like I said, I wanna get the heat off me. Once this gets out, I can slip away and get in the clear."

"Why give it to me? Why not the police?"

Ellis laughed. "Are you kidding? The cops will arrest me on sight. I need someone who's more interested in what I'm gonna give them than actually me."

"And what's that?"

"I can't tell you that. But have you gotten into a Dr. McCord yet?"

"Yeah, his name's come up."

"I'll serve him up on a silver platter for you."

"Where and when?"

"One hour. 2667 West Bridge Street."

"What is that? A house?"

"Some type of office building. It's on the end of a strip shopping center. McCord uses it sometimes to hand out his phony prescriptions. Will you be there?"

"Yeah, I'll be there."

"OK. One hour."

After getting off the phone, Charlotte could tell that something was on Hall's mind. He was just standing there with a weird look on his face, staring at the wall.

"What was that about?" Charlotte asked. Once Hall told her the gist of the conversation, she was more concerned than intrigued. "You're not actually gonna do it, are you?"

"Why not?"

"Because it could be a setup, that's why not?"

"You always think the worst."

"And you don't think enough, apparently."

"I'll go there, see what he has to say, check out the evidence he's got, and that'll be it."

"You can't seriously believe that, can you?"

"Why not?"

"This doesn't smell right," Charlotte said. "This can't be on the level."

"Again, why not?"

"First off, how'd he get your number?"

"Beats me."

"Brandon, this worries me."

"It'll be fine."

"I don't think so. You gotta tell Bradham about this."

"I don't even know what this is all about," Hall said.

"Brandon, either you call Bradham and tell him about this or I will. I mean it."

Hall sighed, knowing he was being forced into a corner. And he wasn't about to make his girlfriend mad. He reluctantly called Bradham to let him know. Hall told the detective everything Ellis had told him.

"Your girlfriend's right," Bradham said. "Ellis was at the scene of a murder. He's a wanted man. Why would you even consider going over there yourself?"

"Well, I know you're tied up at Sharon's house."

"You know, sometimes I think you got rocks for brains."

"Gee, Steve, don't hold back your true feelings or anything."

"Brandon, how do you know this call was legit?"

"Well…"

"And how do you know it was even Ellis?"

"Because…"

"Maybe it was someone else using his name trying to draw you out."

"Well…"

"And how do you know this person is intending to give you anything? Maybe they just want you out of the way and want to kill you."

"Well, it…"

"I think Charlotte's right. It sounds like a setup to me. And you're dumb enough to fall for it."

Hall remained silent, figuring he was just going to get interrupted as soon as he opened his mouth, anyway.

"Well, aren't you gonna say anything?" Bradham asked.

Hall rolled his eyes. "I just figured that you were gonna talk for me so what's the point?"

"The meeting's in an hour?"

"Yeah."

"I'll wrap it up here and meet you over there."

"As soon as he sees cops, he's gonna split," Hall said.

"We'll stay in the background. We'll let you go in and we'll stay on the outside. If anything goes sideways, we'll rush in."

"All right. By the way, how's it looking on Sharon?"

"Could be suicide, could be murder," Bradham answered. "Need to do further testing."

"Like what? Looked pretty open and shut to me."

"That's why we actually investigate. So we can be sure. There was some bruising on her arms, like maybe her arms were being held back. It was recent."

"If it's not suicide, maybe Ellis did it?"

"Anything's possible at this point. That's why you need to be careful here. This guy doesn't have much to lose."

"OK. I'll meet you there."

"Well, let's meet up at the other end of the shopping center first so I know everyone's in position."

"All right, sounds good." Hall put the phone back in his pocket and looked at his girlfriend. "Bradham will meet me there. Happy?"

"Yes."

"I'll let you know how it goes."

"No, you won't."

"Why not?"

"Because I'll see it for myself. I'm coming."

"Charlotte..."

"Don't Charlotte me. I'm coming and that's that."

Hall sighed and threw his arms up. He knew it was pointless to argue. He wasn't going to be able to convince her to stay home. "OK, fine, get ready. We'll leave in ten minutes, I guess."

Both of them got themselves ready and ten minutes later, they were on their way to meet Ellis. The uneasiness in Charlotte's stomach didn't let up the entire drive. She knew there was something funny about this meeting. It wasn't as legit as it sounded. Hall knew it was possible it was a setup. But it was also possible it was on the level. There was no way of knowing until he got there.

Hard Bargain

By the time they pulled into the far end of the shopping center, they noticed Bradham's car pulling in right in front of them. They parked and got out, meeting by the detective's car. They still had about twenty minutes to go until the meeting time.

"The more I think about this the more I don't like it," Bradham said. "We know he's there. Let's just go in and rush him."

"How do we know this isn't some type of test?"

"What kind of test?"

"To see if he can really trust me. Maybe he's watching from somewhere else to make sure no cops are involved."

"Yeah, maybe."

"Let me go in and see what's up."

"OK. But I'm only giving you five minutes tops. Once that's up, we're coming in no matter what."

Hall nodded. They continued talking by the car until it was time to go. Hall got back in his car, alone, and then drove to the other side of the shopping center. He pulled into one of the closest available spots and got out of his car. He cautiously walked toward the end store, but there wasn't much to see. There was some kind of black paper or tarp that covered the windows and door, so he couldn't see inside. Hall pulled on the front door, but it was locked. He knocked on the door, waited for a minute, then knocked again. There was no answer. Hall looked around, then decided to try the back. He slipped around the side of the building, getting to the back door. He pulled on it, and luckily, or unluckily depending on what he would find, it opened. Hall took a few steps inside, finding himself in what most businesses would use as a storeroom for extra merchandise.

Hall looked around, though there wasn't much to see. There was nothing there but some empty shelves. There wasn't a single box or bag to be found. There was another door straight ahead that Hall assumed led to the main part of the store. He walked over to it and opened it, hoping that he might find Ellis on the other side of the door. He slowly opened it, trying to stand to the side in case it was a setup, so he wouldn't be in the direct line of fire. Nothing happened, and he pushed it open all the way. With still nothing but silence, Hall peeked his head out, not seeing anyone there. He then took a few more steps, firmly putting himself inside the store. He looked to his right and sighed, seeing an all-too-familiar sight lately. Two dead bodies on the floor. There were a couple of folding chairs just beyond them, along with guns on the floor. Though Hall didn't recognize one of the men, he instantly recognized the second man as Ellis. Without touching anything else, Hall pulled out his phone and called Bradham.

"You better get in here," Hall said.

"You OK?"

"Yeah. Better call your crime scene unit."

Hall stayed put until Bradham and his officers

came into the building. As soon as the police came in, Hall pointed out the bodies.

"That's how I found them," Hall said.

The police immediately started taping off the scene and getting to work. Hall was taken outside and met back up with Charlotte, and he told her what happened. They stood by the car for a while until Bradham came back out.

"So what's the story?" Hall asked.

"Right now, looks like a double homicide."

"Who's the second person?" Charlotte asked. "The one is Ellis, right?"

Bradham nodded. "One of the victims is Ellis, correct. The other is Dr. Martin McCord."

"McCord?" Hall asked.

"That's right. Looks like they shot each other."

Hall didn't really believe it. "Really? A double homicide?"

"Right now, that's what we're working with. There are powder burns on both bodies, indicating the shots came from up close on both of them. Both guns have been recently fired. Unless we get some prints on someone indicating a third party, it's gonna be near impossible to prove there was another person there."

"Unless there's a witness."

"If there was a witness, I think we'd have heard about it by now."

"Why's that?"

"Because the medical examiner says those bodies have been dead for about ten or twelve hours. That would put it in the middle of the night. Good luck finding a witness at that time."

Hall looked down at the ground, having trouble processing what he just heard. "Ten or twelve hours? That's impossible. Ellis just called me an hour ago."

"Did he?"

"You know he did! I told you about it."

"You talked to someone who said he was Ellis," Bradham said. "I told you it could've been anybody."

"That means this whole thing was staged then. It was designed to bring me down here and find this deliberately."

"Maybe."

"Maybe nothing. Dead men don't talk, at least not the last time I checked."

"The problem is there's no proof."

"You don't need proof to know something."

"But you do if you want it to stand up in court," Bradham said. "I've told you before, there's a difference in knowing something and proving it."

Hall didn't look pleased. He knew this meant the trail was going to go cold. Everybody involved in this case had turned up dead. Everyone except for Rankin, and nobody knew who he was or what he looked like. If he was really the one behind all of this, he was going to skate free. At least for now.

Hard Bargain

It was the day after Hall had found the bodies of Ellis and McCord. It was just after lunch. Hall and Charlotte were trying to figure out their plans for the day. It felt a little weird not having anything to investigate. Hall's phone rang. He eagerly answered it seeing that it was Bradham.

"Hey, what's up?"

"Just figured I'd give you the news."

"What news?"

"Got the handwriting analysis back from that letter you found."

"And?" Hall asked anxiously.

"It's a match for Jernigan. He did write it."

"I guess that does it then, huh?"

"Yeah. The Zeller case has officially been reclassified as a murder, with Guzman and Jernigan implicated as the culprits."

"And the motive?"

"It's going down as unknown. Can't prove anything specifically, and we can't write down theories. But at least it's something."

"Yeah. At least it's something."

"Don't sound so down," Bradham said. "We did good work on this. *You* did good work on this. You're probably the main reason we got all this."

"Just feels like it's unfinished somehow, you know?"

"I hear you. Believe me, all too many cases wind up

that way. I know the feeling. But don't lose sight of the good things either. We found out what really happened to Zeller, and we got four bad guys off the street. I consider that a win in my book. I'd take that any day."

"Yeah, I guess you're right."

"I am. Believe me, I've dealt with this stuff a lot longer than you have."

"Let me ask you something: you really think Rankin might be behind all this stuff?"

"In my gut? Yes. But that and a quarter will still buy you nothing."

"Yeah," Hall said. "I can't help but feel like he's behind everything."

"He slipped away this time. But we'll eventually get him. He'll screw up somewhere along the line. They all do. And we'll nab him."

"Yeah. Just hope it's not after a dozen more bodies pop up."

"What about Zeller's sister? Want me to notify her of the change to her brother's case?"

"No, I'll do it. We'll head over there now."

After getting off the phone, Hall told Charlotte of the developments. Then they drove to Olivia Zeller's house to let her know about her brother.

"How do you think she'll react?" Charlotte asked.

"Probably relief. It'd be hard to be happy about it. But at least she'll know the truth."

Once they got to Zeller's house, they were invited in, and they all sat down in the living room.

"We just wanted to tell you that the police have officially changed your brother's death to murder," Hall said.

Olivia immediately started breaking down. "I'm sorry," she said between tears.

Charlotte hopped over to the couch beside her friend and put her arm around her. "It's OK."

"I just knew he didn't do that to himself."

"Well, you were right," Hall said.

"Why? What happened?"

"Well, there are still a lot of things that are unclear."

"What about the men who did it?"

"They're all dead. I don't know if that'll be comforting for you or not. But maybe you'll find some peace with it."

"Why'd they do it?"

"Nobody knows for certain," Hall answered. "Our theory is that we think your brother might have stumbled into some illegal prescription filling racket. He might have gotten killed to make sure he didn't talk."

"I can't believe it."

Zeller broke down crying even more. Charlotte hugged and held her until she was able to compose herself again. Hall and Charlotte stayed there for an hour until Olivia was back to her normal self again. When they finally left the house, they walked back to the car. Before getting in, Charlotte wondered about their future plans.

"So what are we gonna do now?"

"Well, I got some things to do," Hall replied.

"Like what?"

"This is what I was made to do. I got a license to get."

ALSO BY MIKE RYAN

Continue with the 3rd book in the Brandon Hall Series:

Dark Day

The Silencer Series

The Eliminator Series

The Extractor Series

The Cain Series

The Ghost Series

The Cari Porter Series

A Dangerous Man

The Last Job

The Crew

ABOUT THE AUTHOR

Mike Ryan is a USA Today Bestselling Author. He lives in Pennsylvania with his wife, and four children. He's the author of the bestselling Silencer Series, as well as many others. Visit his website at www.mikeryanbooks.com to find out more about his books, and sign up for his newsletter. You can also interact with Mike via Facebook, and Instagram.

Printed in Great Britain
by Amazon